Transfor...

Write Here, Write Now, and Beyond

by K-12 Teachers in the
Rutherford County, Tennessee
School System

WRITE TOGETHER™ PUBLISHING
Nashville, Tennessee

Published by Write Together™ Publishing LLC.
www.writetogether.com

ISBN 1-930142-54-4 (Hardback)
ISBN 1-930142-53-6 (Paperback)

Title: Transformations: Write Here, Write Now and Beyond. Subject: 21st Century
literary collections; American authors. (Multiple authors).

Project Sponsor: Rutherford County Tennessee Board of Education,
    J. Hulon Watson, Superintendent

Project Coordinators:
    Laura Harper, Assistant Superintendent of Curriculum and Instruction
    Shelia Bratton, Middle Level Coordinator
    Elizabeth Church, Language Arts Instructional Specialist

Publishing Advisor: Paul Clere

Typesetting & Book Design: Charles King

Contents

A Special Place

The Heart of a Child

Heirlooms

Reaching Beyond

Personal Transformations

RUTHERFORD COUNTY BOARD OF EDUCATION
2240 Southpark Boulevard
Murfreesboro, Tennessee 37128
Phone (615) 893-5812   Fax (615) 898-7940

Dear Reader,   August 18, 2000

A remarkable thing happened in June 2000, resulting in the book you are now reading. K-12 teachers from across Rutherford County, Tennessee volunteered their time to take part in *Transformations: Write Here, Write Now and Beyond,* the Rutherford County Board of Education's first Writers' Academy for Educators. The Academy brought teachers together to write collaboratively, to hear from education experts in the field of language arts and wrting, and to swap curriculum ideas on how to best teach writing to K-12 students. The teachers did quite a bit of writing on their own, and techniques such as peer evaluation and process-writing were explored in seminars throughout the week as they looked at writing from the students' and the teachers' perspectives.

I was extremely happy to see the teachers' reviews of the Writers' Academy; they were overwhelmingly positive in tone, and the works of art that came out of the teachers' writing assignments are magnificent and inspiring. We hope that it will inspire you, the reader, to write, and to encourage those around you to be excited about writing.

Best regards,

J. Hulon Watson

J. Hulon Watson
Superintendent of Schools

A Commitment to Excellence

A Special Place

The Bookmobile

I remember how folks in Landers looked forward to the third Tuesday in every month. That was bookmobile day!

You could see the red dust clouds rising from the big black tires under those curving fenders long before you could see it. You could hear the clattery, chattery clack the big green bookmobile made as it climbed over Payseur's Mountain and down the steep hill into our narrow cove.

The cove was a wonderful place for a child. The crawdads and the quick, silvery trout in the cold mountain stream, the pink wildflowers on the balds, and the untamed blackberries growing amid the briars in the pasture all held enchantment for a child. Each morning I traced the outline of the mountains with my finger in the air and recited their names: Big Tom, Craggy Mount, Potato Knob. Into this serene world, on the third Tuesday of each month, came a capsule from another world full of undreamed of people, unfamiliar places, and strange things.

Miss Hattie would bring the bookmobile with its over-heated, hill-worn brakes to a screeching stop outside my grandmother's home and people would appear from nowhere. Women in dresses and aprons, men in overalls, and barefooted children, all eager for a new book. The books were placed in my grandmother's parlor in her tall bookcase. From there, community people would swap out their books. Sometimes Miss Hattie had saved a special book just for me.

I grew up loving a book's rough-textured cover, crinkly rough-cut pages, raveling string edge (hanging from the most worn books), and that cream-colored thread stitched into the center of the book. Mostly, I remember the smell, opening the book, and that soft papery smell wafting up to my nose. If I could have dived into that smell, I would have— hands first, head first, heart first.

When I was very young, I read the books on the bottom shelf, the children's shelf. As I grew taller, I read those books, shelf by shelf, working my way to the top shelf, through the romances, the Rex Stout mysteries, and the Zane Grey westerns. My growth was measured by shelves. What a world surrounded me!

My world changed when I was twelve. We moved from my beloved mountains to a mill town in the foothills: new house, new school, new friends; no mountains, no streams, no large extended family.

Mama, sensing my forlornness, took me to town one afternoon in our '54 Ford. We turned into a paved drive outside a large red brick, white columned building. Huge oaks shaded the lawn. Large pots of red geraniums sat at the feet of two resting marble lions.

We walked inside. That smell! I knew where I was. I was home. A new home, but home.

Rebecca Brooks
Lascassas Elementary School
Fourth Grade Teacher

Stair Poem: Maddie

A dog waits patiently for her people.
Under the dark, dusty tool shed every day
Sniffing, woofing, lounging
Maddie

Rebecca Robertson
Blackman High School
Tenth Grade English Teacher

Square Dancer

Rhythmic music saturates the air
Toe-tapping and hand-clapping to the beat
This dancing is so much more than square

Cheering crowds at the performance
Stage make-up so dark, hair out of my face
Costumes with numerous items to wear

Parades down Main Street in any given town
From Woodbury to Paris, we attract a vociferous mob
I can remember every step of the dances we share

Friends so precious
Partnerships form from necessity
Continuing through a lifetime, anytime, anywhere

Emotions intertwined
Exhaustion, elation, blistering pride
Ache in my head from the braids in my hair

Memories of times when I felt nonpareil
All tucked safely inside my heart
This dancing is so much more than square

Sheryl Evans
Rockvale Elementary School
Second Grade Teacher

I Remember...

I remember turning down the small, narrow lane that leads to my Grand-parent's house. The road, untouched by human intervention for years, seems to stand still in time. Overgrown leaves from the fence-line dance and tickle the car's exterior. Turning off the pit and tar country lane, gravel and dust rise suddenly to hit the sides of the car. I continue towards my destination with the bumping, jarring, and shaking all alerting me to the entrance of "The Farm." Once again, the rhythm changes as the wheels spin into the lazy moving waters of the branch. The branch is a child's wonderland of moss, sparkling water, broken shells and slippery snails all on a bed of flat rock. Mother said the Indians called it Bear Creek. Maybe bears came from miles around to lap the cool waters before retreating into the lush green thickets of the nearby forest. As the wheels once again hit gravel, dust sticks to the tires as evidence of passage through the branch. I can now see the white picket fence in the front of the house. As we cross over the stopgap the yard becomes more visible. The yard. The yard is lined with watermelons grown by my grandfather. Stacked high as humanly possible, the watermelons make a strange pattern of greens against the blue, August sky. Dark greens, light greens, striped and plain.

Movements from the porch, with the screen door opening, reveal a red straw hat, gray hair, and a crooked cane emerging from the depths of the dark house. Pap, my Pap. The car door opens and I scramble out. The familiar greeting from my grandfather is issued with a few colorful words. "Hey Baby, came to see ole Pappy?" Hugs, kisses, and a searching eye for Granny follows.

Walking into the old farmhouse, smells of tobacco, dampness, and supper cooking all seem to invade my senses at once. Overwhelmed by the odors, I gasp a breath of fresh air before entering fully. Granny, apron around her waist, comes sauntering from the vicinity of the kitchen, wiping her hands on her stained, cross-stitched apron.

"Where's your Mom?"

"Moving slowly," I reply softly. My attention returns to Pap who is now smoking on the porch.

I hurry back outside to swipe the cigarette ashes off Pap's shirt where he keeps a constant supply. His T-shirt peeks at me through the many burnt holes in the front of his shirt. As I smear the ashes into his cotton shirt, he yells at me not to get him dirty or Granny will be upset. I think this is really funny because he is already showing signs on his shirt of breakfast, lunch, and two or three fresh cigarette burns. "Do you wanta ride to the back with me, Baby? I've gotta check on my vines. They're almost gone. Better get your pick of the crop while you can."

We head towards the shed, kicking a few of Molly's kittens out of the way, to an old beat-up truck. Thrusting his cane to the back of the truck bed Pap climbs in, cursing the whole time. Climbing inside the cab, I once again inhale fresh air before shutting the door. Pappy lights another cigarette from the fading light of its predecessor and blows the smoke into the already confining space of the cab.

With a thrust of his key, turning the engine, he hovers over the steering wheel as the truck backs down the driveway. More ashes fall to the floorboard of the truck as the steering wheel swipes his belly clean once again.

"Why does he let the ashes build into one long cylinder of gray before they drop to their resting place?" I speculate as I look at his shirt and the accumulation of used tobacco on the floormats.

"Hey Baby, do you need some coke money?" as he pulls a quarter from his pants pocket. A quarter. A large sum of money. I take the quarter and hold onto it tightly, palms sweaty from the August heat. We head up the hill to the back watermelon field. My curls blow wildly about my face while I poke my head out the window for more fresh air.

Forty years later I can still smell the lingering tobacco smoke and see the love in my Grandfather's eyes as I drive up the very same hill, to the very same field where my home now lies. Closing my eyes, I can see Pap rolling the watermelons over to check the yellow bellies of the ripening melons while he quickly thumps the bright green outer skin. "That's gonna be a good one, Baby." Walking away, he turns and smiles at me as he gathers a bouquet of zinnias for Granny's supper table.

The memories are like threads, holding my mind together with the closely-knit weave of love. I scan the field, looking for evidence of Pap's existence, maybe a wayward zinnia, as the tears run down my face. Pappy, I remember....

Suzan Warren
David Youree Elementary School
Second Grade Teacher

Sweet Summer Memories

I remember
the dust of the rugged cotton fields,
the bright green tractors raking hay,
a long, sweltering four-hour drive,
and rickety shacks along the way.

I remember
helping with the garden chores
and wax candy full of juice;
the smell of Aunt Rachel's southern food,
and Archie's dog running loose.

I remember
blue and red rooms where two girls played
and enormous trees which provided shade,
girls in pigtails painted up like clowns,
a Baptist church in a small, sleepy town.

I remember
traveling down the road a piece
to another home full of love;
where a house and barn stood below
and a silo stood above.
Jersey cows were in large supply
and you always waved at passersby.

I remember
Socks the cat, Buttercup the bull, and Checkers the horse
(Black-and-white spotted, of course)
The hours of playing Uno cards
The little garden in the yard.

I remember
the time spent in an old hayloft
Golden straw is so soft.
Hours spent talking with Cousin Ted
And never wanting to go to bed.

I remember
coming home with great memories
of these happy times with family.
The summer days of love and laughter
In my mind now and ever after.

Delann Hickman
Cedar Grove Elementary School
Fifth Grade Teacher

I Remember Charlie

I remember living on my grandparent's farm when I was eight years old. The farm was several hundred acres with wonderful places to play. There were apple orchards, ponds, fields and woods. The house was a stucco monstrosity that had once been a gambling house. My mother told me how the steel double doors (which had given the gamblers time to escape during raids by the police) had to be removed when she was a child because they were too heavy for her to open. There were so many rooms in the house most of them weren't even used, except for storage. The room just off the huge living room was the room where I slept. The logs from the original house were still visible on one of the walls. Compared to the other rooms in the house, this one was small.

When the weather was bad, I played in the house. You could get lost for hours with all the rooms and crawlspaces. I used to look all over for sacks of leftover money. Surely the gamblers had left some behind during a raid. Occasionally, I would find some coins or a dollar bill lying around, but I think it was my grandfather's doing. Still, even into my teen years, I searched. I just knew there were bags of money hidden somewhere in that house.

I was most happy when I was outside. I was only eight and a girl but I had been given free reign to wander as I pleased from the time I was about five. Back then, it was safe for little children to play unsupervised. I rode my pony, Chigger, almost constantly. I had pony paths all over the farm. I fished and tried to catch turtles in the ponds and swung from the barn loft onto Chigger's back like a cowgirl movie star. My grandfather set up little jumps, logs really, and barrels so I could pretend I was in a real horse shows. I watched the tumble bugs and tried everyday to catch the snake that lived in the fence row in the back field. Spittle bugs made egg-white froth on the plants but I imagined it had dripped off the slobbering jaws of the many rabid animals that seemed to wander through our fields. If you rubbed the froth with your fingers (which was unwise unless you wanted to catch rabies yourself) you could see the little black bugs. I knew it wasn't really rabid dog slobber, but it was fun to pretend.

In the late sixties there was a rabies scare in the area. It seemed that every skunk, fox and stray dog had rabies. The technique back then was to kill the suspicious animal, cut off its head and "send the head off" to Nashville where the brain tissue could be tested for the deadly virus. We had lots of dogs, cats and just about every other kind of animal on the farm so my grandmother and mother were understandably concerned about me playing alone too far from the house. I was restricted to the yard for awhile. I was playing with my rabbits one day, pretending they were babies and "feeding" them with baby bottle carrots. My uncle's old dog Shep, who was my constant companion, was standing guard beside me. Suddenly Shep growled. He was looking toward the road where two strange dogs were wandering in the front field. We were supposed to report strange animals, so I ran to tell Grand Daddy. They shot the dogs and sent off the heads. The results were positive. Rabid dogs. Almost in the front yard! Rabies seemed to be all around me. Reading *Old Yeller* a few weeks before hadn't helped.

As long as I could remember my father had raised beagle hounds and hunted with them. One beagle, Charlie, wasn't much of a hunter so he just ran around loose and was a pet. Charlie had survived distemper as a puppy but the disease had caused him to have seizures or "fits" as my grandmother called them. She thought he was possessed. One day while my grandmother was hanging clothes on the line I was trying to teach some little kittens to ride on Charlie's back. All of a sudden, Charlie just fell over in a fit. The kittens ran under the porch and my grandmother rushed me into the house. Later, when I snuck back outside, Charlie was running around the yard playing. I was sure he wasn't possessed.

One morning, a red fox was lying dead at the entrance to the garden. The poor thing had electrocuted itself on the electric fence that was supposed to keep animals out of the vegetables. My grandfather had the fox stretched out on the picnic table. He let me touch the beautiful red-orange fur. The fur was soft and damp from dew. The long tail had a big white tip on the end. While I was admiring the fox, the men were discussing how odd it was that the fox would have come so close to the house. I didn't think it was odd at all. I knew the fox's den was in the old apple orchard near the garden. She had two babies. I saw them all the time. I kept the information to myself. Maybe I could feed the baby foxes now that their mother was gone. I knew the little foxes would have to be tested for rabies if anyone knew about them so I kept the information to myself. Grand Daddy told me to go back to the house. I knew what was coming.

By this time my grandfather just took the heads to Nashville himself. It was faster than waiting on the game warden to come. A few days later we got the call. The fox had been rabid. Even at the age of eight I reasoned that it was unlikely that every strange animal in Manchester had rabies. My grandfather admitted that maybe the test wasn't very accurate but it was better to be safe than sorry. The vet came and vaccinated our animals for rabies. I was sure it was too late for that.

By now our dogs were tied or stayed in pens. The cats and Shep were allowed to stay in the house. Poor Charlie was tied to a doghouse. Whenever he saw me, he would jump and bark and strain at the end of the chain and, even though I'd been told not to, I sometimes untied him so we could play. One day he went off to chase rabbits and didn't come back for a long time. When he came home, I scolded him for running off and tied him back to the doghouse. He whined and howled as I walked away. At supper that night Grand Daddy asked, "you didn't untie that dog today did you?"

"No sir," I lied.

It took me a long time to get to sleep that night. I could only think of the baby foxes and rabies. I felt guilty for lying to my grandfather.

9

I tossed and turned. I counted the logs on the wall of my little room. I finally fell asleep with my hand on Shep's head, thinking about poor Charlie, tied outside with the rabid animals...

Beside the bed Shep was growling...

Charlie was snarling and snapping his jaws, straining against a short chain attached to the wall of my bedroom. Long strings of slobber hung from his snapping jaws. He was jerking at the end of the chain and growling. His angry eyes stared vacantly. He did not recognize Shep or me. Suddenly the chain broke. Shep tried to protect me but Charlie was across the room and on the bed in one leap. He sunk his teeth into my right leg. I screamed. Shep barked.

My parents ran into my room. I was screaming and clutching my leg where the pain shot through. Shep was worriedly licking my face. I told my father that Charlie had rabies and had bitten me on the leg and that now I had rabies too. I tried to show them the bite on my leg but the gashes and blood were gone. My parents told me I'd just had a bad dream. They assured me that Charlie was fine and asleep outside in his doghouse. They stayed with me until I fell asleep.

The next morning Shep and I ran outside. Charlie was barking and wagging his tail, straining at the end of the chain attached to his doghouse. He was ready to play. I went to the barn where my grandfather was working on the tractor. I don't think he really believed there was a rabies epidemic anymore than I did. I'd also found pans of food at the entrance to the fox den. I figured it was my grandfather's doing. He knew I was tired of playing in the yard and riding my pony in circles in the barnlot. He said I could untie Charlie and go to the big pond (the little pond by the barn was just to water livestock and didn't have any fish in it). I untied Charlie, got my fishing pole and we all went fishing.

I sat on the bank of the pond, line in the water and watched Shep and Charlie running in the field, noses to the ground, their tails wagging. Chigger dozed under the big sycamore tree. There was a tug at the end of my fishing line. I was happy.

Candy Swan
Oakland High School
Biology Teacher

"Showtime" in the Funeral Home

One of the most interesting and fun things I did during my childhood was to put on musical shows with my friends and relatives. We used whatever was "at hand" for props and costumes, although my Mother kept a box of old clothes and shoes specifically for "dressing up" purposes. Since I played the piano and was always taking lessons, this was a perfect backdrop for "dramatic activity." These shows took place at home, on the sidewalk, in another friend's house, or wherever the mood struck.

One of the most fun places we put on shows was in my uncle's funeral home! This may seem morbid to some, but it wasn't to us, because the funeral home was located next door to my cousin's house, and it was easy to run next door.

There was a room in the back of the funeral home containing an old upright piano. This was in the back room, not the rooms where funerals took place. I might add that the funeral home was in a Victorian style house that had been redone. We sang and danced to whatever tunes were popular at the time! This room was entered through the embalming room, about which we thought nothing, since we came through it all the time, and it was at the back of the house. I was very familiar with the embalming room, and it didn't bother me at all!

We also used the area for the choir as a stage, and whoever was playing with us at the time would sit out on the floor in the front and watch the performers on the choir box. I played the organ, and sometimes we played "church" with whatever hymnbooks that were available.

The most interesting backdrop that we had was the "bier," which was behind the area where the casket would be placed during a funeral. It was a grouping of very heavy draperies and unusual Victorian lamps. This was really the best place to perform, since we could control the lighting and pretend that the curtains opened and closed.

At one point in time, funeral directors used a very large piece of "netting" to drape over an open casket. This material had a wide border around the edges and came in several colors. We took those and attached them to our hair with bobby pins. They made beautiful "bridal veils" which trailed behind us like a "bridal train," since weddings were also part of our dress-up fun. I'm sure that my uncle did not know about this, nor did he know about our "hide and go seek" in the casket room!

It was great fun to play that game in the casket room. Everyone hid, however many were playing; the lights were turned out, and the "seeker" came in to try to find anyone he or she could find. Once, I found one of my relatives lying in a casket as his hiding place! There was much screaming and laughter!

My uncle allowed his daughter to drive the hearse— one of those old, lumbering, big, black things, across town to get the gas tank filled. We didn't need any money because she just said "Daddy says 'Fill it up.'" I rode with her several times, and this was before she had a driver's license! We could barely see above the dashboard. After doing this, we would play "hearse ride" in our dress-up clothes in the hearse and she would "pretend drive."

The hearse had a large, powerful spotlight, which we would shine at night across the street at the upstairs window of the "little watch man." He would wake up and raise the window and shake is fists at the air, not knowing where the light was coming from. At that point, we would cut the light out. The "little watch man" was a homeless man who sometimes fixed watches for people in town and was inebriated most of the time.

Another fun thing that we did on the back porch of the funeral home was to ride on the "casket carrier" up and down the porch. It was on rollers and had wine-colored velvet drapery material hanging down from the bars. It made a great car! Sometimes we had shows outside that porch, as it was secluded from the street. Other times, we played house in the front sitting room with its lush, squooshy Victorian sofas. Being small, when you sat down you "sunk" into the cushions.

It was a fun time! Nobody knew we were in the funeral home— at least we thought they didn't — and it was cool and dark. We thought it was great! I never had any dreary or sad thoughts about playing there. Those were some of the "best shows" of my "early dramatic life!"

Betty McClure
Thurman Francis School
Sixth Grade Teacher

A Legacy Lost

Everyone in my family called them Ging-Ging and Pa. In high school, I remember some of my friends' mocking of their names—"You are going to see your Ginseng this weekend?" But their joking didn't bother me. My beloved grandmother was Ging-Ging, so termed by one of the first grandchildren who couldn't manage to say the formal term grandmother. And my grandfather was Pa—without a "w." My grandfather typified the stern, strict disciplinarian. I look at pictures of him today and am amazed to see this open smile across his lips. I don't remember him smiling—ever. But my grandmother was different. I loved the aroma of her freshly baked coffee cake, the cinnamon filling and sugary frosting, some wonderful concoction I haven't ever been able to recreate. My grandmother loved me completely as all grandchildren need—no rules, no frowns, just love. Today, as an adult, I hear veiled undercurrents from my mother and aunts about the guilt and resentment felt for their mother at times. But, of course, this is the complex nature of mothers and daughters and granddaughters. To me, my grandmother was the one person who would buy me that chocolate chip cookie when Mom warned me "no more sugar," and she was the one who encouraged me to follow my dream even without the assurance of career stability. My Ging-Ging.

My grandparents retired to Waverly, Tennessee, living in a home near Kentucky Lake where my Pa could wake at 5:00 A.M. to fish those early-rising bass. I loved their house. It became a second home to me after my parents' divorce. My sister and I lived there several summers while my mother finished her education to return to teaching. Surrounding the home was a wraparound porch overlooking the golden Kentucky Lake. Sometimes my Ging-Ging would let me sleep on this porch—such an exciting experience for a ten-year-old. Even though I slept on a hard, cold pallet, it felt like a feather bed to me. If I were forced to sleep in the house, I slept upstairs, waking up to see little dancing rays of sunshine on the ceiling like pirouetting ballerinas. My sister and I would run down the rock steps to Pa's boat dock, jumping at last in that clear, cold water. A mimosa tree grew outside the front door and the little, pink flowers would float down our backs as we ran around the yard. We were always barefoot. All the family would gather there in the summer at some point—my cousins, aunts, uncles—there must have been fifty of us altogether, with my Ging-Ging clucking over us, offering iced tea and warm towels.

When my Ging-Ging sold that place after Pa's death, I was fourteen, too young to realize what was gone. Then, several years later, my Ging-Ging died, too. My favorite cousin, Dick, remarked at her funeral that the reason for our family to get together was also now gone. I was sure he was wrong. When I turned twenty-one, Dick returned to Tennessee after being gone for a long time. He suggested one afternoon that we ride to Waverly to see Ging-Ging and Pa's home on the lake. I was so excited, so anxious to recall those joyous times. We drove over two hours to reach that idyllic haven, and as we drove up the driveway I was shocked. The shutters were cracked, falling off their hinges—those green ones my Pa was so meticulous about. The mimosa tree had been cut, leaving just a hacked stump. The once so carefully placed rocks leading to the boat dock were jagged, misplaced pieces of some incomplete puzzle. And that boat dock—all rusty and unkempt—some unwanted and neglected child. Certainly the people who lived here now were not grandparents. Dick and I walked around wordlessly for just a few minutes and just as quietly got in the car to drive off. I have never been back since.

Jill R. Walls
Smyrna High School
Eleventh Grade English Teacher

Blooms

Golden rolls of hay
Lying on emerald fields
Southern summer's blooms.

Ginger Hartlein
Christiana Elementary School
Eighth Grade English Teacher

Marriage

It was July 24, 1993,
the hottest day of the year.
It had rained only five minutes before
our pictures were taken.
The steam was rising like the sun in the Eastern sky.
My husband and I had just said, "I do!"

We were both exhausted and tired.
We waited impatiently for the photographer's snap.
Sweat and half-hearted smiles have overtaken us.
We were ready for cake, drinks, and most of all air conditioning.

Our family and friends were gathered to help celebrate this special occasion.
So much to look forward to, like children, holidays, and creating a
    happy home.
All I can think now is how young and naive we both looked.
Both of us knew at that moment we had found our soul-mate and we
    have regretted nothing since.

Shannon Lowe
Rock Springs Elementary School
Fourth Grade Teacher

Wet Muddy Pig

Wet muddy pig
Gobbling slop voraciously
Colorful art, playful statues
Lovingly, collections evolve.

Janet Quarles
Rockvale Elementary School
First Grade Teacher

Summer

Hot sultry nights
Raining only slightly
Sun-parched gardens, hot days
Simmering summer descends.

Wanda Jones
Smyrna West School
Kindergarten Teacher

I Remember Farm Life

I have surprised many people who think they know me. My appearance at times speaks "city girl." I love hats, dressing up, shopping, eating out, and visiting exotic places. My father-in-law, who owns and runs a farm, thought I was too "citified" for his son. Little did he know that some of my fondest, earliest memories came from a farm much like his own.

When I was between the ages of four and six, my parents and grandparents owned a farm they managed together. Since I was a young child, that farm seemed huge and awesome. I wandered many a day over its limits looking for adventures that only a young child seeks.

My sisters and I were fascinated with shows about Dr. DooLittle and *Bonanza*. Our interest spilled over onto the farm as great scenes from the shows were acted out. We seemed to be caught up in a magical world safely hidden among the trees and shrubs that lined our place.

Granny Ruth, my dad's mom, had a huge garden and yard. Fresh vegetables were picked right off the vine and tasted. My kindergarten class found comfort in Granny's shaded yard, and on numerous occasions you would find my family cranking homemade ice cream and swapping stories in that yard. The porch swing, the ham curing house, and the chicken yard are still vivid images of a simple life securely hidden in the farm's confines.

Life was not always perfect as I lived those good old days. I remember vividly a bull attacking my dad. The blood that drenched his clothes still haunts me at times. Once, our hay barn caught fire on a very hot summer day. I was summoned at my young age of five to stand in the front yard and direct the fire trucks to the back barn. The smoke that billowed out from the barn, the anxiety of my family over the great loss, and the commotion that ensued has forever endeared to me persons who suffer personal loss from a calamity.

One special memory I have concerns the horse my dad bought me for my birthday. I was so excited to be the owner of such a fine steed, particularly since I was only a kindergartner. Daddy had some of the farm hands help me learn to ride. I was led around the yard and taught the vocabulary needed in conducting a horse. Dad and my trainers then decided that I must ride solo around Granny's house. My family sat on the large porch and waited. I remember thinking "Wow, this is really neat, but this horse is not moving fast enough." (It is funny how such obscure things stick out in your mind over the years.) To solve the speed problem, I dug my heels into the beast's sides and with all the voice a child of five could muster, I instructed the animal to "Giddy Up." With a relieved spirit, my horse obliged and set upon his own course of action. As I passed my parents at a speed that seemed supersonic, I knew I was in trouble. They ran out to help me. Just as I felt safety would once again envelop me, the horse gave a giant leap, and I fell haphazardly onto the sidewalk. I was scared and felt none the worse except for the pain that was touching my subconscious mind. Later that evening, after a rough time going to sleep, my parents realized I had suffered a broken arm. I still remember the ER and the doctor who sang "How Great Thou Art" as he set my arm in a cast.

I never saw that horse again. Daddy felt somehow responsible for the whole episode and decided that such an animal was not befitting his young daughters' needs. The event had a great impact on my life. I have just recently gotten back on a horse for the first time since the accident some thirty years ago.

My life now is not similar to those days on the farm. I don't own a large garden, a hay barn, a horse, or even a hand-crank ice cream freezer. I do own, however, those memories, experiences and opportunities that remind me I am not "too citified."

Marzee Woodward
David Youree Elementary School
First Grade Teacher

A Heart's Home

The car exits the interstate, negotiates traffic through the edge of town, and turns onto a narrow road leading away from the city limits. Shortly, it turns into a gravel driveway, and the difference in the texture of the ride and noise causes a small gray cat to venture from his place under the driver's seat beneath me and hurry to my lap to peer out the window. We make the curve end of the long driveway, and the car stops with Obie pawing eagerly at the door. We are home.

That home to which we have come is one in which the cat has never lived beyond the visits he and I make on occasional weekends, for he and I are city dwellers, studiously involved in the activities at graduate school, the city itself, and our small apartment. (Obie is perhaps a more dedicated student than I, since he spends a great deal of time draped across open books and papers, while I try to spend as little time as possible even considering said books.) Now I wonder why he loved the farm on which I was raised; being of a romantic turn of mind, I like to think he could feel my security when I was there and took it as his own.

Physically, my home is somewhat nondescript. The seventy-five acres of the Manson Pike are divided into three fields with a few acres commandeered by a red brick house, a somewhat wooded yard, a hopeful orchard, and an occasionally prolific garden. But my real home is a compendium of images from the tiny kitchen, to the grove of trees I grandiosely called the forest, to the big bed on which I and my big brothers spent six weeks of afternoons talking to my recuperating mother and playing cards and board games or doing homework. It ranges from the hideously cracked asphalt at the approach of the house to the rose bushes, irises, day lilies, and other plants which my mother has coaxed along for thirty-seven years. It is the mound of huge rocks, presumably piled by an earth-moving machine when the pond was dug, on which I would climb as a child and feel very adventurous indeed. It is the unbelievably uncomfortably bathrooms that are always cold and have never seen a shower head. It is the creak in that door at the top of the stairs and that funny light in the upstairs hall that can only be turned on when its companion switch is on at the bottom, necessitating many a trip up and down. It is the well-worn fireplace in the den and its almost pristine sister in the living room, and it is even the unadulterated mess of books and papers on the bookshelves that line the den walls. I don't remember a time when the shelves were cleared or even tidy — my father worked best in melee, apparently, and my mother, patient and longsuffering, adapted to his system.

I have my own home now. It is all the things the house on Manson Pike will never be. It has a shower and a manageable yard, and it is smack in the middle of town. I can walk to church, to the bank, to the post office, and to the grocery. I revel in its conveniences. But Obie the cat has chosen to make Manson Pike his home in fact and in heart, and enjoys roaming the fields and sleeping on the breezy screened porch. Like my little cat, that home is still paramount in my heart, and it is still my first thought when events of sorrow, joy, or just plain tedium crowd my day. Progress has now lumbered down the Manson Pike, stopping to build myriad subdivisions as it goes. Last year, it even installed a traffic light. But in my mind's eye, the land still stretches across the pike in virginal state, the window units still have to be hauled into the house each summer, and my family still talks, sings, argues, and loves, frozen in youthful isolation.

Mary Catherine Sevier
Oakland and Riverdale High Schools
Spectrum Teacher

Willow Tree

Pretty soft willows
Swaying limbs below
Green leaves, feathery stems
Quietly they flow.

Susan Wade
Roy Waldron School
Third Grade Teacher

Summer

Blistering summer days
Flies buzzing annoyingly
Humid weather, cold watermelon
Lazily, time elapses.

Leave
In an orderly manner
Not shrieking or shuffling
Down the corridor
At dismissal.

Linda Postiglione
Roy Waldron School
Third Grade Teacher

An Unforgettable Christmas

Christmas is the time set aside for celebrating the birth of Jesus Christ. It is also the time for families to get together. My family is no exception. As small children, my brother, sister, and I would stay awake as long as our little eyes would allow us. We would whisper about the presents we wanted and about what we might get before drifting off to sleep. When my brother died, Christmas took on an even deeper significance. It marked a time for our family to reflect on his life and support one another at the same time. I know my brother loved Christmas and would have been disappointed had our family not continued to celebrate Christmas together. So for the past 28 years I have spent Christmas with my family. Even after moving to Nashville, Tennessee with my new husband, I still made it a point to somehow return to Florida to be with my mom, dad, sister, and niece. I was determined not to let this tradition end.

This past Christmas was full of surprises. Derrek, my husband, and I were all set to go to Florida, but a change of plans halted our vacation. Derrek works for Columbia/HCA where he is responsible for correcting and fixing computer errors at hospitals. Due to the Y2K pandemonium, my husband's employer decided it would be best if he stayed and worked throughout the Christmas break. Upon hearing the news, my heart dropped like a ton of bricks. After recovering from the shock I decided to do what every girl knows how to do best. I called my daddy. My daddy comforted me and reassured me that everything would be all right. Deep down in my heart I knew this was true.

About two weeks before Christmas my sister called to inform me that she, my niece, and my parents were going to travel to Tennessee for Christmas. I was amazed to hear this because my parents never go anywhere. The fact that my sister was coming was even more amazing. My sister has Sickle Cell Disease and rarely gets out—especially to another state. The smile on my face was as broad as the Golden Gate Bridge. My dad had come through and I was going to spend Christmas with my entire family after all. I knew this would be a Christmas to remember.

Two days before Christmas my family drove up in a rented mini van. Derrek and I ran anxiously out of our apartment complex to greet them. What a reunion! It was as if I hadn't heard from them or seen them for years. I was overwhelmed, happy, excited and even in awe at their arrival. They had actually come and had made it safe and sound. Those days were filled with laughter, shopping, cooking, decorating, and relaxing. It was as if I was back in my childhood home. On Christmas Day, we arose bright and early to attend church. We worshipped together as a family giving thanks to the LORD for his wonderful, unspeakable gift—his son Jesus Christ. After church we returned home to put the finishing touches on Christmas dinner.

Little did we know that my mom had already cooked everything! It was a feast that I had remembered from past Thanksgiving and Christmas holiday meals. There were ham, turkey, green beans, macaroni and cheese, candied yams with melted marshmallows, rolls, desserts, and dressing. My mom's dressing is the world's best. I couldn't wait to taste it. I could feel my mouth watering just thinking about the dressing. As you can imagine the kitchen in my apartment was not that big, especially considering the amount of food being cooked. When it was just about time to eat, my mom took the dressing out of the oven and placed it on the stove (all cabinet-top space was occupied). Unfortunately, the eye on the stove was still on! We heard a sizzling sound and then... there was a huge explosion of glass and dressing. The look of disappointment on our faces was unspeakable. Talk about mixed emotions. It was so funny but, at the same time, I was crushed. In desperation, I begged my mother to let me pick around the glass to get just a taste. After much pleading and reasoning it became clear to me that the dressing I had yearned for was to be left untasted.

On the evening of Christmas Day my parents loaded up the van to return to Florida. As they pulled away, thoughts of our time together drifted through my mind. I saw my niece running around, my family together in church praising the LORD, my mother's kind smile, and I heard my dad's warm laughter. I even remembered the Great Dressing Disaster. At that moment I knew I would never forget this Christmas. The 37" television set and stand given to us from my parents could not compete with the sweet Christmas memories I will treasure always. I remembered the many sacrifices my parents had made so we didn't miss Christmas together. Then, for a fleeting moment, I saw a smile of pure joy on my dear brother's face as he watched from above.

Lisa Kegler
Rock Springs Elementary School
Fourth Grade Teacher

The Lawn

Frosted, fragrant lawn
Buzzing with a grist of bees
Clover blooms abound.

Ginger Hartlein
Christiana Elementary School
Eighth Grade English Teacher

The Heart of a Child

Old Sam

I remember Old Sam. He was an old, blind, gentle horse, long-ago-retired from the daily grind of his work on the farm. The old hired hand, also gentle, also long-ago-retired, whose name was not important to a five year old, was faithful and always there to guide Old Sam on his way.

The farm where Old Sam lived belonged to my family's friends, Moody and Georgia, a couple who were also old, gentle and long-ago-retired from their daily grind of farm work. Although this farm was, for the most part, retired, a menagerie of ducks, chickens, goats, dogs, and cats still lived there with Moody, Georgia, the hired hand, and Old Sam. It was a treat for this city girl to visit the wonderful farm with all of its unfamiliar smells, sights, and sounds, and I would beg my parents to take me to see Old Sam again and again.

The hired hand (I do wish I could remember his name) would pick me up and place me on Old Sam's back. Carefully and slowly we would be taken on a snail's-pace ride around the pasture near the barn where Old Sam lived. Old Sam's blindness did not keep him from knowing the way, but the ever-faithful hired hand who loved children, but especially loved his Old Sam, gently led us on the ride, which lasted no more than five minutes and was over all too soon for me. Old Sam was unable to go any farther—he was too old and weak to carry me any longer. The rides on Old Sam were the highlight of my visits to the farm, and of all the animals— the ducks, chickens, goats, cats, and dogs, I loved Old Sam the best.

During the early years of my childhood, my parents worked part time as ushers at the Ryman Auditorium in Nashville. One weekend Roy Rogers and his horse Trigger were performing at the Ryman and, of course, Mother and Daddy were working and, of course, they took me with them to work. I was thrilled to see my favorite "singing cowboy" and Trigger in person. After the performance we went backstage to see my heroes.

A stagehand gently lifted and placed me on the magnificent, famous Trigger's back. As I sat in the saddle of the most famous horse in America with his finery of silver, fringed reigns, and engraved leather, I was not the least bit impressed. When asked by Roy Rogers, this famous movie star, who was himself a gentle, kind man, how I liked his Trigger, his famous, impressive horse, my reply was, "I'd rather have Old Sam."

Pattie Johnson
Rock Springs Elementary School
Seventh Grade Language Arts Teacher

Daughters

Giggly, zany girls
Creating havoc quickly
Freckled face, sweet smile
Gently, mom hugs.

Marzee Woodward
David Youree Elementary School
First Grade Teacher

Jake

Just when I think you are
A holy terror, you throw a
Kiss in my direction and I'm once again
Ensnared in your sweet baby innocence.

Laurie Jobe Watts
Christiana Elementary School
Fourth Grade Teacher

The Special Day

I remember feeling the sun as it beamed down upon my face. It was a fresh spring day. Yes, I remember. The day is pressed in my mind. It was April 12, 1976. I know the day, not because it was my birthday, but it was the day Grandaddy was buried.

I remember the smell of the cedar trees and honeysuckles as they perfumed the air on top of that hill where my grandfather would finally rest. I had never attended a funeral, let alone a funeral on such a special day as my birthday. I remember being so excited about the presents and cake, yet feeling so much emptiness for someone so close being gone forever. I remember the touch of my mother's hand on the small of my back as she soothingly whispered, "Everything'll be all right. He's with Jesus, now." I had forgotten about my special day as the preacher uttered such things as "Pearly Gates" and "Streets of Gold." I wondered if with all these things that he'd miss me as much as I'd missed him. I wondered if my special day would become a day best forgotten.

I remember the sound of heavy silence filling the car as we drove home. I began thinking of who would sneak me candy at Granny's house while Momma would fiercely protest or who would lift me those three extra inches to reach that branch that all the other kids would easily climb. I remember wanting him back.

Finally, I remember the taste of chocolate icing and the sight of flickering candles. I recall the capgun, the cowboy hat, and the bigwheel that had been shelled from their wrappings. Over the cake, I noticed the same people that I had seen before, still clothed in the same raiment as on top of that hill. I caught my father's gaze; our eyes connecting. He smiled for the first time that day, and we both realized that Grandaddy would always be with us.

Michael Hickman
Rock Springs Elementary School
Fifth Grade Teacher

How to Save Our Young Girls from Sadness

Why does our society continue to negate and lower the value of women? I see it when we start "prettying up" girls too soon with make-up instead of letting them be children. I see the madness when children are birthing children. I get angry when the media force our girls to grow up too soon. They are not allowed to develop into one being; instead, society is geared toward finding mates for them and having them accept roles as defined by society. Why can't we let each person grow into his or her own self so everybody matures into an individual first, mate second?

Take a poll of fourth, fifth or sixth grade girls and ask them what they want to be when they "grow up". A high majority of them will give a concrete response: nurse, teacher, police officer, or librarian. But something happens to these goals by the time the girls begin the "social dance." Too many girls are bombarded with messages from print, TV, music and parents that they must learn how to attract the opposite sex. True, all animals must mate to continue the species; however, my contention is that, as a society, we are forcing our girls to enter that part of their lives too soon. With the emphasis on pre-mating skills, our girls are losing their dreams and their goals. How can they be whole entities and have individual strengths if they are so concerned with the primary skills needed to take a mate.

I don't want my students, and the ones who follow, to be the women who "sit in sadness" because they played society's game too early in life. I want to help them be strong and recognize that they themselves come first. Girls need to learn that their first responsibility is to themselves so they have the ability to earn a living by themselves.

Jan Wadleigh
Smyrna Middle School
Eighth Grade Language Arts Teacher

I Remember Fourth Grade

I have a fourth grader's soul. I am they, and they are I. Of all my years in school, it appears that it was the fourth grade and my tenth year of life that made a significant imprint upon my memory. The flashes of memories long past are not always school scenes. However, the evocation of this time revolves in and around that happy period of my life and fourth grade.

My thoughts move to a patriotic play where *I* was the Statue of Liberty. Even today when I hear… "Give me your tired, your poor, your huddled masses yearning to breathe free," I am called back to that young girl wearing a draped sheet, holding aloft that glorious aluminum foil flame holder and wearing the matching crown. Who could know that so simple a presentation would continue to have impact nearly 50 years later?

Do you recall the pygmies of Africa? I do. Even today I cannot think of these exotic people without "seeing" their thatch-covered houses in the black and white photographs of my "modern" textbook. Africa was, to me, as distant as Mars and as familiar. I often wonder if the social studies lessons I teach today are nearly as memorable?

It was in fourth grade that the world of music was opened to me. This was the year we had class piano. Imagine a class of thirty or so ten year olds playing silently on our cardboard keyboards. Oh, the joy in being chosen to come to the *real* keyboard and hear the keys actually respond beneath my fingers.

Other scenes play softly in the recesses of my middle-aged mind. The ten-year-old girl riding a bike anywhere and everywhere, playing hide and seek with friends after dark, playing with my highly treasured telephone switchboard, and myriad other pleasures of an innocent, joyful time waiting to be remembered.

Ah… memories. Wouldn't it be wonderful to live in the light and aura of childhood one more time? With gratitude in my calling, I get to bask in the daily presence of "God's people" — 4th graders. Fourth graders enjoy the glorious crown of childhood. It is truly a golden time. I believe teaching is the next best thing to going back.

Elizabeth Bouma
Homer Pittard Campus School
Fourth Grade Teacher

The Miracle of Hayden

There are moments in life that, by their very nature, you know are going to be life-altering. They are the obvious kinds of events. But even these events have their surprise effects. They often swirl like waters overflowing their confining boundaries into the far corners of your mind, transforming even the darkest spots into illuminated wisdom and understanding.

Hayden Jackson, my grandson, was born on March 30, 2000. Hayden is actually my stepgrandson, but as love looks on, lines, definitions and restricted roles blur.

I married Hayden's grandfather almost twelve years ago. That is when Missy and Michelle, his two daughters, came into my life. Because of unforeseen circumstances, these girls would be my experience of motherhood. By the grace of God, I am blessed with a warm and loving relationship with each one of them. So when Missy called long distance that hot July day to share with us the news of her pregnancy, I felt blessed at the prospect of a grandchild.

With blended families, roles never seem to be clearly defined. I realized early on in my relationship with my stepchildren that I needed to be sensitive to their perception of me as their stepmother and father's new wife. I also soon learned that I needed to be aware of their mother's vulnerability. I tried not to impose myself or to step over lines of perceived territory. I learned to step back, to wait, to see where I would best be placed. I have also learned to live with a certain amount of uncertainty. Over time, I have grown to know my value as a member of this family without having to have a clearly defined role.

It seemed as though I went through an accelerated form of this process when I learned that Missy was pregnant. I struggled with such issues as what the baby would call me and if I would be accepted as something more than Grandpa's wife.

This stepparent ambiguity seemed to magnify when Missy called to ask if we wanted to be called when she went into labor regardless of the time, day or night. My husband had the assurance of the ruling class, not even having to question his sense of rightness in this situation or his sense of belonging. I, on the other hand, struggled with the appropriateness of my place. We came to a decision as a couple that we both wanted and needed to be there.

28

So, we put the baby's due date on the calendar and started planning our life around the arrival of Hayden. He was officially due three days before my spring break, and one day before I was to have the cast I earned on a field trip on my left wrist removed. I prepared sub plans, alerted my fellow teachers, prayed that I would at least have my cast off, and waited.

Missy's due date came and went. So did the rest of the week, and then the weekend. Still no Hayden. Her doctor finally set a date for inducement. It looked as though Hayden was going to need some help with his arrival into the world.

Hayden was set to appear sometime during the 24-hour period of March 30, 2000. We knew Missy was set to go to the hospital early that morning. So, we set out for Cookeville early that day anxious to be there, yet apprehensive at the possible awkwardness of the situation. As to be expected, her mother was going to be there and there were often feelings of uncomfortableness between my husband and her. As we arrived at the hospital, we said a prayer asking that everyone involved be blessed.

We walked into the hushed, darkened labor room immediately aware that Missy was sleeping between contractions. She was hooked to all of the latest instruments, gauges, and machines to assist in a process that was as old as time itself. Her mother was there at her bedside with full focus on her daughter. Missy's husband, Brian, hovered like a humming bird back and forth around the bed. I knew immediately that this was one of those events in life that allowed flawed human beings to reach down and tap into what is strongest and best about themselves. We were all there for Missy and Hayden and this common bond encircled all of us canceling anything else.

Shortly after we arrived, Missy experienced another contraction. We all snapped to attention like soldiers on a battlefield. She started practicing her breathing as she had been taught, looking brave and determined, with the pulse of Hayden from the monitor echoing in the background. Not long into it, though, the brave, confident 26-year-old dissolved into a scared, whimpering child who wore a look of bewilderment. It was if she saw her misshapen body for the first time and was looking to us to explain how and why it happened. Her mother was stationed at the end of her bed on a cold, metal stool massaging her daughter's feet while my husband and son-in-law acted as braces for her to rest on as she searched for a comfortable position. All the while, the quiet, dark room and the rhythmic background heartbeat continued to hold us in a somber, subdued mood.

By 11:30 the doctor came to administer the long overdue epidural. Because of the mistake by this initial doctor, Missy suffered complications all afternoon and into the evening. We were often shooed out of the room by the businesslike manner of the nurses so they could go on attending to the business at hand. We often found ourselves gathered in the hall, staring at the door, willing it to open with relieving news: "Missy's dilated." or "It's going to be any moment now." or "The epidural is doing its intended work." Instead we heard "The epidural is not working, Missy is not dilated. We may have to do a Caesarean."

I could see the three of us, her mother, her father and myself, ready to step forward at a moment's notice to take the pain from her, to erase the worry from her forehead and to perform this feat for her if needed. Instead, we rung our hands, wiped our eyes, and waited.

Missy was finally given a third epidural and this one did its magic. Within a short time her body was finally able to relax enough for her to do her intended job. Within the hour, Brian was out in the waiting room to inform us that Hayden made his arrival. He weighed in at 7 lbs. 6 oz. and was 20 ½ inches long.

When we were finally allowed to see them, Missy was collapsed in her bed with Hayden nestled comfortably in her arm. He was sound asleep after his traumatic experience, secure in the fact that he was surrounded by the people who loved him best.

Hayden came to visit yesterday afternoon. I had him draped across my chest, sound asleep. His mother was comfortably lounged next to us and his grandfather gazed affectionately from across the room. As I looked down at this little body, I realized once again that relationships are not defined by blood lines or circumstances. They are defined by availability, attention, acceptance and understanding. When these ingredients are stirred into a relationship, the result is a love that is unshakable.

Felicia Searcy
Homer Pittard Campus School
Third Grade Teacher

Son

Special son
Proudly
Embodying
Everything we
Dared to dream
Yesterday and today

Ginger Hartlein
Christiana Elementary School
Eighth Grade English Teacher

Essence of Basketball

The final bell rings and an explosion of junior high students floods the hall. As I walk toward the lobby, I am suddenly struck by the smell. In junior high school, there are a variety of smells. Fortunately this is a pleasant one—popcorn. The buttery smell triggers a reaction in my stomach, not one of hunger but of excitement. The popcorn machine in the concession stand has begun its work for the night, which can mean only one thing—a home basketball game. I turn and push open the heavy metal doors guarding the gym. Another smell greets me—the *gym* smell. A mixture of basketball leather, wooden bleachers, and sweat socks is a smell that triggers memories. Emotions of victories, defeats, effort, luck, and lessons learned are blended in those memories. I can almost hear the fans cheer, the squeak of the players' shoes, the swish of the net, the cry of the coaches, and the buzz of the scoreboard. I cross the gym floor, noting that it needs to be swept, and head toward the locker room. Anticipation builds. Will we be ready? Will I be ready?

Pulling open the locker room door, another smell envelops around me. This one is not so pleasant, but very distinct. Polyester uniforms, sweat socks, damp towels, athletic tape, and medicated muscle cream create this strong mixture. This is a room of preparation, excitement, self-examination, and of prayer. I pull out the rack of basketballs and roll them toward the gym.

I feel the anticipation and anxiety that comes before the game. I know the plays, the drills, the strengths and weaknesses of the players, the strategy for tonight's game, yet I am not a basketball player. I am the *coach's kid*, manager of the team, and sometimes, in my own mind, the assistant coach. I've spent two nights a week in a gym during ball season since I was two weeks old. Basketball is a part of my family's life and something important that I share with my dad. I may not be a player, but I am on the team. I give heart and soul to the team just like my dad. Dad and I always make an excellent team.

Whenever I walk through a gym today, I am suddenly struck by the familiar smell and am transported back to those basketball days. I remember the sweet victories and the buttery popcorn. I can't really remember a specific game or team, except the team of Dad and me. Fortunately, we are still a team in many ways today.

Monica Helton
Cedar Grove Elementary School
Fourth Grade Teacher

The Lefty

Backward, awkward hand
Writing words clumsily
Difficult tasks, untied shoes
Quickly she adapts.

Pattie Johnson
Rock Springs Elementary School
Seventh Grade Language Arts Teacher

Grandaddy

I remember everything about Grandaddy. He lived to be eighty-two. I was thirteen and in the eighth grade by that September; I remember well because this was the first time I ever saw my father cry.

Grandaddy never seemed to change. I think I would have noticed as my grandparents were our neighbors, and we shared everything on the farm. In my earliest memory, Grandaddy had thick, soft white hair, and crystal blue eyes behind small circular wire-rimmed glasses. He had the kindest, gentlest face I have ever known. He seemed almost boyish as he enjoyed every facet of everyday life and all of those around him, including the animals. Even each morning was a new beginning for Grandaddy, as Granny directed him to wear the neatly pressed khakis and the light blue or white starched shirt. His generous smile and quick wink said "thank you" as he tucked the fresh white handkerchief in his pocket and sat down to breakfast.

On one particular June morning my three sisters and I were visiting in my grandparents' kitchen as we often did. Grandaddy sipped the last of his light chocolate-colored, cream-filled coffee and asked, "Have you girls seen Honey today?" We thought about it and revealed that we had not seen our favorite plump, yellow cat in a day or maybe two. This might mean she had finally chosen a perfect hiding place to have her kittens. The excitement of that idea followed us to the front porch and lasted until we reached the bikes at the end of the sidewalk, and then we had to decide who would ride first — the four of us shared two bicycles. Two would ride or race while the other two watched and cheered and laughed. This competition could go on for a while, as it did that morning, until we heard Grandaddy call for us from the porch, "Joanne, Mary Sue, Lucy, Laura," where he sat in his motionless rocker, smoking the unlit pipe. I heard him first so I motioned for my sisters, who stopped riding and come running; we always did when Grandaddy called. As I reached the end of the sidewalk at the porch steps, I could see Honey in Grandaddy's lap. The entire scene seemed pretty typical at first... Grandaddy in his rocker with Honey in his lap on the big farmhouse front porch. But there was something different; Grandaddy's smile had turned to laughter as he looked down

33

to proudly admire and presented the four brand-new yellow "mewing" kittens that honey had had in his lap. She chose a place she loved and the safest place she knew.... Honey felt what we felt about our Grandaddy.

Mary Sue Persons
Blackman High School
Ninth Grade English Teacher

Bright, Tiny Faces

Violas
small, delicate
growing, blooming, enduring
bud, blossom, infant, youth
smiling, laughing, loving
innocent, resilient
children.

Lisa Bogle
Rutherford County
Elementary Coordinator

The Heathen in Me

"Surprise! Look what I brought home!" shrieked Denny as she entered the apartment late one breezy summer afternoon. In her arms, squirming to get out, to get down, or to get somewhere, anywhere else but trapped in her arms, were two of the most adorable kittens Melanie and I had ever seen. The three of us had knelt in the floor for hours frolicking with them when we realized "Kitty 1" and "Kitty 2" wouldn't work forever.

Denny rationalized that we needed to give them suitable names. Her statement reminded me of T.S. Eliot's "The Naming of Cats" where he explains, "The naming of cats is a serious matter." Well, truly it is.

In fact, it's sort of like naming a blond child Ebony. A name for a cat needs to serve several purposes. It must be short enough to screech in piercing tones, it must suit his or her personality as the owner experiences it, but most importantly, it must suit the cat in question. Cats are quite meticulous in nature and will not readily answer to a name that was chosen without thought or without their approval.

One of the kittens was silvery-gray, and the other black with only a few dots of white on her paws and ears. Both were females; imagine five females living in one apartment! Female felines preen more than female humans, not to mention relaxing more and taking up the majority of space in the bed; after all, the bed and all other comfy furnishings are their territory. Still, even with these generic cat qualities, we didn't want to name them generically, so we waited and we watched.

The first few weeks of their entrance into our lives, they caused so much commotion! They scrambled around the VCR (getting stuck in the process); they ascended the curtains, plummeting far below onto our innocuously sleeping heads. They scaled our clothing to the heights of our closets, stretching and pulling thread heedlessly as they explored every texture, every tone of our fashionable wardrobes. They crawled into the trashcans, turning them over on top of themselves, frequently howling piteously to be released from their dungeons. Of course, daintily nibbling the leftovers was a common occurrence, too.

Over those weeks, we toyed with many names. None seemed to fit exactly. Finally, we decided on Heather for the gray kitten because of her coloring and the softness of her fur. But that still didn't seem right — it didn't portray the mischievous, playful nature of this adorable kitten. It sounded like she was docile and sweet, and we all knew that was only in her dreams, not ours.

That's when we realized — not Heather, but Heathen! It was so perfect! It was affectionate in the way that you call your little brother or sister names like Ijit or Snothead. Most importantly, she answered to it, and she could really be a little Heathen at times. Her sister, the food thief and lounger, readily became Hoodlum.

This is how my darling gray Heathen earned her name and her place in my life. For the most part, Heathen stayed with me her entire life, with the exception of the dreadful time when she disappeared for over three months after a tornado demolished our home. Again, she earned her name. She lived a happy, content, and quite spoiled life before succumbing to a fatal illness last summer. She is gone now, but her memory lives on in my heart. She is undoubtedly "the Heathen in me."

Lois McGonigal
Blackman High School
Ninth Grade English Teacher

Linda's Touch

Roy Rogers was very proud of his new shoes. While riding on the plains, a mountain lion attacked him and in the ensuing scuffle chewed up his new shoes. Having killed the mountain lion, Roy threw the animal across his horse and rode into town, passing the local saloon. A drunk coming out of the saloon was heard to exclaim "Pardon me Roy, is that the cat who chewed your new shoes?"

Sung to the tune of "Chattanooga Choo Choo," these words sound silly; but they provided laughter for my family throughout my sister's battle with cancer. Even now when I hear the song, I mouth these words instead of the usual lyrics.

Twenty-two years ago, my younger sister Linda was diagnosed with acute leukemia. We were devastated. Linda was referred to a hematologist, an excellent physician who was also known for his impersonal detachment. First appearances were not reassuring. He always wore the same pair of black, houndstooth pants and runover shoes. Even worse, Dr. Roy never smiled, but he had met his match with Linda.

Shy, innocent Linda immediately chipped away at Dr. Roy's crusty exterior. She always greeted him warmly, each time demonstrating her quiet confidence in him. The nurses marveled at his response; his gentleness seemed to protect and shield her as a father would his own child. A special rapport grew between cheerful patient and serious doctor. Linda never complained and never questioned the outcome, no matter how sick the chemotherapy made her. Somehow, her trust in him was enough.

So it was that when I first heard the Roy Rogers joke, I rushed home to tell it to Linda and my parents. As I told the joke, I could see the mirth dancing in Linda's eyes. She couldn't wait to tell Dr. Roy. On her next visit, she excitedly told him the joke. He laughed only dutifully at first; but then with greater understanding of Linda, he laughed more robustly. Others might view it as a trivial incident in his busy day. To them, it became another shared moment in that four-year struggle. During Linda's remission, their relationship continued to reveal a more human side of the doctor. To the moment of her death, he remained a guardian of her happiness and comfort.

Few people ever saw the Dr. Roy that we came to know; but for my family, he will always be the Roy whose cat chewed his new shoes.

Elizabeth Church
Rutherford County
Language Arts Instructional Specialist

Billy

His name was Billy. He was five years old with a limp shank of blonde hair that was determined to block his light blue eyes from the world. He came the first day of school in brand new midnight-blue jeans that looked as if they had come straight out of the package that morning and a plaid shirt buttoned all the way to the top. Staring a hole into his brown, leather shoes, he seemed unaware of the untied laces or the classroom around him.

The other children wore shorts, T-shirts and quick, shy smiles for their teacher and each other. But it was as if those untied shoe laces had somehow crept into the tile floor of the classroom because Billy stood rooted to a spot on the side as the other children roamed the territories of their new classroom to discover glimpses of the school year ahead of them.

Did his year improve? Did Billy blossom and grow dear to the hearts of his classmates and teachers? No. Billy is the child my heart aches for and my prayers turn to often. I don't know where he is or if his other teachers ever see the sweetness of his rare smile or the blazing intelligence in his eyes when he does open the shutters to his inner self. Most days that year, he wore those same jeans to school until the midnight of the blue was scarred with pink knees peeking out at the middle, white socks at the bottom and dark multi-colored stains splattered everywhere.

Did I love him enough that year? Did I give him enough hugs and smiles and encouraging words? Did he learn to clean his own face, neck and arms before coming to school? Has he learned to wash and put on clean clothes each day so the odor doesn't form a barrier between him and the other children? Does he still have a sweet smile and shy, blue eyes, or has he put a cold steel lock on his heart?

As long as we have teachers who open their hearts to the young, emerging souls in their classrooms, there will be Billys to haunt us through the years and wake us from our summer reveries. I don't just pray for Billy and those like him; each fall, I also pray for his next teacher... that she will see the possibilities and not ignore them. I want her or him to push aside that lank hair from his eyes and show him the world that awaits him if he chooses to see.

Sarah Jackson
Rutherford County
Middle Level Instructional Specialist

My Grandma and Grandpa

I remember the joy of my grandparents and their enduring enthusiasm. They always greeted me with excitement as if I was their one and only grandchild, though they had thirteen. My childhood was rich with playful moments and bits of wisdom passed down from them.

I remember Grandpa and Grandma running to meet me as Dad would slowly pull our car into their driveway. Their eyes would beam with arms open wide just waiting to squeeze me close. I felt as if my heart would leap from my chest with anticipation of what our days to come would hold.

I remember sitting on Grandpa's knee, combing what little hair he had on his head or pretending to cure all of his ailments with my trusty plastic nurse's kit. He was always so patient as I prodded and pulled on him throughout our proverbial playtime.

I remember Grandma playing for hours with me and comforting the cold of my baby doll Susan. You would have thought she was a fellow six year old herself!

I also remember Grandma's camphor-soaked ears and Mary Kay-slathered face pressed close to mine as she would share some tidbit of knowledge. Even through the distraction of odor and smudge, I could hear her express how much God loved me and had big plans for my life.

I remember both Grandpa and Grandma sharing life's little instructions in such a way that the smallest child could understand. I eagerly clutched onto every word because, after all, they must know it all.

I remember growing into a teenager and somehow believing they would be around forever, until one joyous day turned into sorrow. My sister had just been married by my grandfather (who, by the way, was also a minister). Two and a half hours after the ceremony, Grandpa suffered a massive heart attack.

I remember stepping into the emergency room in disbelief of what was occurring. I stared at him and the cold metal table he sat on. I thought to myself and trembled, "Do I run, cry, scream? — What do I do? — This isn't fair, God!"

He gazed with such peace into my eyes and softly said, "It's going to be okay, honey." These were the last words he said to me or anyone else before he fell dead into the doctor's arms.

I remember the grief that followed and the feeling that my heart was being ripped from my body. The grief was given a whole new meaning as I watched Gradma's mind drift away because of Alzheimer's disease. She became very distraught and confused as she endlessly searched for Grandpa.

I remember Grandma and me switching roles from adult and child to child and adult. Her last days were bittersweet. One minute crying, the next laughing. I often thought how ironic it was now that I was the one talking to her as if she were a child.

Two years after Grandma passed away, Grandma joined him in Heaven. This time it wasn't expected but, instead, a joyous reunion for the two of them.

I remember many things about my grandparents and the endless joy they brought to my life. Not only did they shower me with their love, they taught me about God and his endless, matchless love.

Angela Jackson
Rock Springs Elementary School
Fifth Grade Teacher

Celebrate

I am four years old and it is my birthday—
Wearing a dress made by a grandmother who watches me play
from her heavenly rocking chair.
Playing with my new doll who talks with me in a voice
only I can hear.

A hot, humid August day.
The dress clinging like a woolen blanket —
Smiling for a picture but wishing for a cool drink.
Ready for ice cream that has just finished cranking.

How many days until I am five?

I don't ask "how many days?" anymore…but I am thankful for each one I

Celebrate

Edie Emery
Barfield Elementary School
Seventh Grade Language Arts Teacher

Jade

Holding you in my lap
A perfect fit,
A smile hidden behind your lips
Like a secret,
My baby, my younger self.

Sleepy eyes open wide
At the world,
Cautiously you grow and grow,
Childlike secrets withered,
Gone,
My baby, my younger self.

    Laurie Jobe Watts
    Christiana Elementary School
    Fourth Grade Teacher

An ABCD Class

Angelic students
Bubbling with joy
Constantly striving to please
Dazzled by each girl and boy
    An eager teacher I will be

    Angi Morgan
    McFadden School of Excellence
    Fifth Grade Teacher

Priceless Memories

Memories are more precious than gold. They lie deep within, yet so close. We choose to hold on to some that give comfort like a fuzzy bear and often have a difficult time releasing those that bring us sorrow. In my life, I have chosen to fill myself with as many positive memories as possible in order to create an environment for my husband and children where love is the common thread that is woven throughout our family.

One of my earliest memories is that of clean sheets. Even today when I climb into a freshly made bed, my mind returns to my childhood when my mom changed the sheets each Saturday, and I climbed into that wonderful-smelling bed. I felt loved, cared for, and guaranteed a good night's sleep.

As long as I remember, my church family has been an integral part of my life. My family was always present at what seemed to be every function. From ice cream gatherings after Sunday evening services to week long vacation Bible school, we never missed an opportunity to gather with our extended family. One particular Sunday morning, I flushed my brand new white tights down the toilet. Guess what. My mom and dad took me to services anyway. That memory has put a smile on my face many Sunday mornings as I hurried my own children out the door.

Since the majority of my memories center around the wonderful family that raised me, I have tried to create some special memories for my own children. One of my absolute favorites (and it is my children's also) is "junk food night.' It involves choosing what you want to eat at the store, spreading a sheet on the living room floor and having a family picnic. I love to see their faces when "junk food night" is declared. It is one of those wonderful memories I choose to recall when everything else around me seems to be going wrong.

Pictures of the mind are what keep me going. Some say pictures are worth a thousand words. I say a memory is priceless.

Kathy West
Lascassas Elementary School
Fourth Grade Teacher

Celebration of Life

Foreshadowing dark days ahead, a large dark-colored mole...
Demanding immediate removal and radical reconstructive surgery,
    The doctor's chilling prognosis—melanoma!
Pouncing viciously upon my intuitive suspicion,
    Denial—a best friend during an appalling revelation,
Revisiting past memories of Dad's incredible physical and spiritual strength...
Praying that God's love and grace would sustain his survival and recovery.

The passing of another year, the dreaded reoccurrence—
    A large suspicious lump on his neck!
Acknowledging the bleak days ahead, our ritual of hope, more prayers,
    surgery, and even a longer recovery period.
Generating enormous anticipation and excitement,
    Our youngest sister's engagement to be married in the new millennium!
Replacing our anxieties with countless wedding niceties—bridal shops,
    Wilton cake books, and honeymoon travelers' guides soothing our fears.
Abounding in prayer and rejoicing in God's grace and mercy,
    Daddy's Little Girl
    will be escorted down the aisle on June 24 by our blessed Daddy.

Donna Kay Trobaugh
LaVergne High School
Ninth Grade English Teacher and French Teacher

A Mother's Nightmare

When you become a parent, your life changes as well as your perspective on the important things in life. No longer are you the center of the universe, but that small bundle of joy that you've waited for for months, sometimes years, becomes "the Universe." You envision who this child will look like, what color hair, eyes, and tone of skin he will have, how much he will weigh, and most importantly you hope that he will be healthy. This was constantly on my mind.

On April 24, 1998, I gave birth to a beautiful 8 pound 2 ounce redheaded baby boy. He was perfect and healthy. I wrapped him in a blanket and took him home to join his older brother and the rest of the family.

During the next three months, I spent the summer immersed in every moment with Noah and his 2 1/2 year old brother, Dylan, because I knew that school would be starting soon, and I would not be spending as much time with them.

One night two weeks before school was to start, Noah woke up with a temperature of 104. We had been at the funeral home the day before, and Dylan had been to "mother's day out" so I thought he had picked up a germ from someone. Either way, a 104 temperature was extremely high, and it scared me. However, having been a first-time mom already I didn't get on the phone right away and call the doctor; I should have. Instead, I gave him some Advil and waited for the temperature to break. I held Noah in my arms the rest of the night, and I specifically remember removing his socks and blanket from him so that the heat could escape his body. He felt so hot that if my hands were ice they would have melted on contact. Kind of like when a cool rain hits the hot asphalt on a hot summer day and you can see the steam rising in the air.

Two hours later I checked his temperature again, and it was still 104 degrees. I had noticed that every time I moved him to nurse he would scream as if he had been pinched really hard, but his appetite had not changed. His temperature remained the same throughout the night. I had called the doctor on call that night and he had instructed me to see the doctor in the morning.

That Sunday morning I took Noah in to see the doctor, and after examining him and asking me questions, he instructed us to report to the Vanderbilt Children's Emergency Room for precautionary reasons, never mentioning to me what he thought was wrong with Noah. I called my husband at home, and hardly being able to speak, I told him to meet me at the hospital. All the way to the hospital I remember crying and my heart beating so hard and wondering what was wrong with my baby because the doctor had not told me what he had suspected.

When I reached the hospital, the doctors immediately placed us in a room. Soon after, my husband and father-in-law showed up. The doctors then told me what Dr. Doak had suspected, meningitis. Telling me this was the same as telling me that my three-month-old baby was going to die. I had a cousin years earlier who had had bacterial meningitis and had been in a coma for days, almost losing his life. I knew exactly what they were talking about; I needed no explanation, just lots of prayers, and God.

I suddenly broke into tears and felt very faint. I got a sick empty feeling in my stomach that I have not had since that time. If you have ever been stricken with unexpected bad news, you probably know the feeling I am talking about. As I sat there and watched as they did a spinal tap on Noah, all I could say to myself was, "This cannot be happening to me, God. Why me?"

It took two doctors to do the spinal tap, and I remember the way he lay on the table. One doctor tightly held his arms and legs and literally bent him into an arch. Noah was screaming blood-curdling screams, but I could do nothing about it.

Of course, there was no way I was leaving the room, because I was his mother!

When finished with the test, they sent the spinal fluid to the lab and started an IV so that the antibiotics could get into his system. All I wanted to do was hold my baby and pray to God that the doctors were wrong.

The test came back positive! "God, what do I do now?" I asked. We had to remain in the hospital until the doctors could determine if he had bacterial meningitis or viral meningitis. The nurse wheeled us to our room, which had a note on the door that said, "Isolation, wear masks." That note did not make me feel any better about the situation.

I remember the room smelled like a dentist's office, and it was very muggy. There was a large baby bed with wide metal bars, not like the cute ones seen in the baby department at Toys R Us or Babies R Us. It looked like a mini jail for babies. The nurse came in and made sure we were comfortable and said she would bring some toys in for Noah to play with. I couldn't even tell her what he liked to play with.

When the doctors came in, they all had masks. It made me think of M*A*S*H, which I didn't ever watch. They asked the same questions over and over and over. They would come in day after day and tell me that they were still unsure about the results but that if bacteria hadn't grown yet he's probably going to be fine. I wanted results!

After three days, the doctors determined the Noah had viral meningitis that had caused a virus in his membrane and an extremely bad headache. My husband could relate because six weeks previous to Noah's birth he had undergone brain surgery due to a chiari malformation of the brain, which was causing him migraine headaches. I was overwhelmingly relieved that Noah was okay, and I never wanted to see a hospital again. Yet, I was so grateful that my husband and child had survived something that could have been very tragic.

I have learned to take one day at a time because of this experience.

Tracy Townes
Rock Springs Elementary School
Sixth Grade Language Arts Teacher

The ABC's of an Elementary Teacher

A—A room full of smiling faces
B—Bright opened eyes glued to every mistake I make
C—Construction paper creations made just for me
D—Dozens of unfamiliar faces each new school year
E—Enthusiasm over each new day
F—Fingers moving up and down to add and subtract
G—Genuinely being told, "You look just like my Granny, she died."
H—☺
I—Imitators, playing school and sounding just like me
J—Jingling lunch money thought lost but found in the other pocket
K—Knots in shoelaces that only I can untangle
L—Love notes saying, "I wish you were my mommy."
M—Melodies of "Happy Birthday to You"
N—Never ending questions from inquisitive minds
O—Opportunities to make a difference in a life
P—Popcorn parties on reward day
Q—Quieting a noisy classroom after recess
R—Rustling graded papers

S—Sticky homework papers that little brother wrapped his sucker in
   last night
T—Tattle-tails from 8:00-3:00
U—Unique personalities placed in one classroom for an entire school
   year
V—Victory in conquering the unconquerable
W—Wishing that Christmas, spring and summer vacations would
   come around sooner
X—Xerox copy fumes floating through hallways
Y—Yesterdays that are now precious memories
Z—Z-Z-Z-Z-Z-Z-rest tonight for tomorrow is a whole new day

Jeanie Medlen Barrett
Christiana Elementary School
Second Grade Teacher

Sam

Anxiously awaiting the arrival of my sweet son, my dearest friend
Debbie and I made our monthly trek to Nashville for haircuts. The baby
was not due for two more weeks, but with my inability to be punctual
with anything and that great motherly instinct, I knew the baby would
not be on time either. However, as I watched my newly cut hair falling
to the ground, I had an incredible pain in my side. After a few moments,
it passed, then there was another pain. I got up and walked around.
This one passed also. Five minutes later, another one. Debbie, being
omniscient, knew I was in labor, but I, again with that motherly instinct,
just knew I could not be. I had heard about typical labor and back labor,
but never side labor.

Apprehensive, we left Nashville for home. It wasn't long before I was
intensely crying, "Oh God! Oh God!" Debbie, the incessant planner,
reminded me to call my husband Rob. I could not locate him at work
and he was not at home, so I was forced to leave him a message on our
answering machine. I listed each item to be packed in my bag and told
him to meet us at the hospital.

We got to the emergency room and were quickly admitted — screaming women aren't too good for P.R. Once in the labor and delivery rooms, the nurses hooked me up to all kinds of machines and monitors. As Rob walked in the room, something went terribly wrong. The nurses wheeled me out while putting an oxygen mask over my face and were talking about an emergency C-section. I looked into Rob's and Debbie's eyes and saw fear and paralyzing thoughts of, "not again," which they tried to mask with looks of bravery and calmness. They knew I wanted terribly to be a mommy and were extremely afraid for my sanity if God chose to take this child, too. The baby's heart rate had dropped dangerously low, but then, miraculously, came back up. We would go through this two more times before the doctor decided the baby had toyed with us enough and proceeded with a C-section. Finally, after the loss of one son and the frantic arrival of Samuel Brooks Gardner at 6:04 on January 4, 1997, I was "Mommy"!

Michelle Gardner
Lascassas Elementary School
Fourth Grade Teacher

My Son

Running, skipping, jumping
Over the creek boulders to visit
Buddies, uncles, a cherished grandmother.
Energy abounds.
Rivers couldn't stop
This almost nine year old.

Rebecca Robertson
Blackman High School
Tenth Grade English Teacher

Heirlooms

The Silver Band

A simple piece of jewelry holds a lifetime of memories. The silver band on my right index finger goes unnoticed by most, but I glance at it often. My thumb glides over it naturally as my mind wanders to another place and time.

It is September 26, 1998, we are all flying frantically around my grandmother's house. Hairspray spritzing, make-up strewn on the bathroom counter and my mother's voice calling out, "Is the veil straight, does it look okay?" For the hundredth time my aunt, my grandmother and I reply, "Yes, of course." Surprisingly, we manage to get dressed without strangling one another. Today is my mother's wedding day. My father died four years earlier due to cancer and my prayers have been answered for her to encounter someone to share the rest of her life. During the chaos, my grandmother calls me into her bedroom to give me something. She lays the half-inch, gold-lined silver wedding band in my hand and closes my fingers tightly around the ring. She tells me that it has been years since she wore the band and thought I would like to have the ring. Of course, I ask why she did not give it to my mother or aunt? She simply says, in her grandmother way, "Because I wanted it to be yours."

The music plays softly and our dear family and friends anxiously await the bride. My brother Jason and I stand nervously on the steps as I share with him the day's events and the gift. He holds the ring and comments on how nice it is. He tells me I should have my father's name engraved on the inside of the band because of the width. This way it can represent both sides of my family. As I exclaim, "What a great idea!" we are summoned quickly inside because the wedding is starting!

A week passes until I realize I don't have the ring. I am devastated and terrified to admit to anyone that I have lost the precious gift. I retrace my steps; search my bags, purse and car. Unwillingly, I give up the search and plan to tell my grandmother the news at Christmas.

December 25, 1998, Christmas dinner at my grandmother's I am stuffed to the gills and scared that I must soon tell of my sin. Jason asks me to come outside because he has something to show me. Outside, he pulls a ring box out of the glove compartment of his truck. I am thinking he is going to tell me about proposing to his girlfriend, when, low and behold, there is my grandmother's ring. He places the ring in my hand and closes my fingers tightly around the band. He says calmly, "You left this in my jacket pocket at Mom's wedding." I am relieved beyond words, and no one but he and I know the ring was ever missing. I thank him, we hug and he drives away.

This is the last time I will see Jason alive. He is killed April 1, 1999, in a car accident. It is only then that I remember his suggestion about engraving the ring. Sadly, now I have two names to be forever imprinted inside the silver band.

The ring is a simple, silver band, a piece of jewelry from my grandmother. Some day I will give it to my daughter or granddaughter as a family heirloom. However this keepsake means much more. It represents my grandmother's commitment to her husband, her love for her children and grandchildren and my love for my father and brother. This band, however unnoticed by others, means everything to me. It represents all that I am and will forever hold a lifetime of memories.

By Kimberly T. Malone
Barfield Elementary School
Sixth Grade Teacher

Reflection

The ivory-backed mirror was dented with age and as yellowed as a full moon. Its shape reminded me of my baby spoon, only bigger. Standing before the old dresser on which it had rested when I was a child, I picked it up, gently turned it over, and observed my reflection in the beveled looking glass. In an Alice-like whirl, I was drawn into the mirror and dropped into childhood, hearing my great Auntie Boo saying, "be careful now, don't break that. It was my mother's—it can't be replaced." And, very carefully, I would take down an antique blue music box and the yellowed mirror, and play pretend games, which only lonely little girls can possibly understand. Now, the funeral was over, Auntie Boo was gone, and I was back, holding the memory of that long-ago child, as I gazed into my old, ivory mirror.

Nancy Bradshaw
Homer Pittard Campus School
Second Grade Teacher

An Heirloom of the Heart

She only appears dimly in my memories. But on my ring finger, closest to my heart is a simple, gold band that spans time and proves she was a real and dynamic person. She was my grandmother, Gladys Inez.

Sadly, my most vivid memory is from the night she died. As was common in the forties and particularly the rural south, she had walked to visit her daughter and grandchildren along a small, country highway connecting the two homes. I remember she held and rocked me and stayed until we fell asleep.

Upon leaving and very close to her home, she was struck and killed by a drunk driver. She left a family of seven children and a husband. She was 47.

Recently, my mother gave me her simple, gold band, and it is the only real connection I have to this woman I would love to have known.

She was strong, quiet and talented, or so I'm told. She played guitar and mandolin with her brothers and sisters, perhaps while wearing this ring. I'd like to think I inherited a small portion of her talent.

My granddaughter will receive the ring next. Hopefully, she will carry out some of the unfulfilled promises of a life ended too soon.

Elizabeth Bouma
Homer Pittard Campus School
Fourth Grade Teacher

The Magical Spoon

As a little girl, I was mesmerized by my grandmother's china buffet. Every piece of China fit perfectly into its own little place and always looked immaculate. I knew that every piece in that cabinet must be extremely precious because it stayed locked behind glass most of the year except for special occasions like Christmas or Easter.

One thing never, I mean *never*, came out from behind the glass, so it must have been the most valuable of all. Nestled in its own little nook between the large gravy boat and the sugar dish sat a shiny little baby spoon. It seemed to always catch my eye and I would just stare at it and wonder what babies my grandmother might have fed with it. The baby must have been someone important for her to have kept the spoon this long. It was enclosed in a small rectangular blue box with a clear plastic cover. The spoon had a little horse standing in front of a rainbow at the top and a little dangling state of Missouri below. It must have been a baby from Missouri, I would daydream… maybe a prince, princess or someone even better! I used to spend hours imagining what could have happened with the spoon and where all it had been before finding its resting spot in the china buffet. The mystery was very exciting.

My grandmother died when I was eleven years old. When my mother began to pack up the china, I slowly reached up, took the tiny spoon from its resting spot and held it for the first time. I hugged it and left the room. I think that my mother noticed, but knowing my fascination with the spoon and my grieving the loss of my grandmother, she let me go without saying a word.

From that day until now the tiny spoon, still in its little blue box, the plastic slightly yellowed from the years, has had a new resting place on top of my dresser. It is there to remind me of the wonderful times I had pretending and creating fantastic stories about the magical spoon. Every time I look at it I can't help but smile, and remember my grandmother smiling at me as I daydreamed about the spoon in the china buffet.

Annette Holloway
Smyrna Middle School
Seventh Grade Social Studies and Language Arts Teacher

Legacy

The lead soldier, his head fallen off, lay on the floor.

He was one of the many positive memories my mother left me. He was a memory of how she tried to raise her children as thinking, reacting, imaginative, and independent young people. Television was unknown in our house at the time. I was in the fifth grade, and my parents had just gotten divorced. As I grew up, money for everyday toys was scarce, but the little lead soldier, three inches tall, in Revolutionary War garb, was one of our play toys.

He, along with four other sets of armies, a farmhouse and accompanying animals, and various naval ships, comprised our toys. I still remember the forts my brother and I made out of the wicker chairs and the dingy pink blankets that served as our battlefields. We each got two armies but it didn't matter to us that they were representing different eras: Civil War, Revolutionary War, and World War I replica soldiers. All we wanted to do was determine a winner. We took turns moving our men, either five singles or the entire corps at a time. In retrospect, I think we played a game that was a combination of chess and checkers. I learned how to surround the bad guys, double-up men, and to anticipate moves my brother might make in future turns. Maybe the skills I learned back then helped me be a ponderer.

These lead creatures that had belonged to my mother in her childhood became her gift to us. Other kids in the neighborhood would be indoors watching television on those rainy, cold or snowy days, but we played, stretching brain cells as far as we could. After each battle was over, we would replace the fallen soldiers' heads and equipment, and place them between the layers of cotton in the wooden box. They were treasures to me: their painted little faces, some wearing mustaches, with their detailed uniforms and paint-tipped dots serving as buttons. Mother shared a tangible part of her youth, but the intangible gifts were a real legacy.

Jan Wadleigh
Smyrna Middle School
Eighth Grade Language Arts Teacher

The Wedding Band

Pure as gold
never ending,
dented, not broken.

Engraved with a promise,
worn in honor,
given to a daughter.

Bringing hope,
a child's marriage,
expecting a blessing.

> Kathy Cotton West
> Lascassas Elementary School
> Fourth Grade Teacher

The Steinway, My Grandmother

Crackled, chocolate finish; smooth ivory keys; blunt, angular legs; flowing, curved body; warm, fuzzy hammers whose job it is to strike cold, metal strings— the Steinway possesses many opposing characteristics. It smells of time.

The piano stayed in its room, the piano room, alone. I would go there to play and to escape. Did my grandmother do the same thing? Did she feel the same way when it belonged to her? Did she have reasons to want to escape her life as I did?

Jane, my grandmother, a woman I only know through a few select photographs, has remained a figure of mystery. My mother never talks about her mother; she died when I was only three. I remember my mother lying in bed, and I remember her crying. I don't remember her ever talking about Jane. Mom does display her mother's picture in the room with the piano. Her skin is smooth and flawless; her lips are curved; her teeth are angular; her cheeks are full and round; her eyes, exotic, almost oriental in nature, are a deep chocolate brown. How can I be related to her? What other characteristics did she possess? Was she a person who gave warm, cozy hugs? Probably not, says intuition. Was she a woman who was striking, yet had a coldness, which rang through her like the piano's metal strings? Is this why my mother never talks about her? I think of the piano; I think of her.

The piano connects her with me. In my mind, her essence is embodied by the piano. I imagine the chords she played, and the emotions that once danced over the keys. The sounds that must have come from the piano echo in my mind. The silences that loom from her photo ring in my ear.

Heather Stewart
Buchanan Elementary School
First Grade Teacher

What's in a Name?

Kathilu. A good southern name, as my mother used to say. So
different in the sound and spelling. *Kathi* with only an "i"
and *lu* without the "o." Misspelled, mispronounced, so different!
One name, not two, pushed together to avoid a middle name.
Kathilu — named after both grandmothers to keep the peace.
Katherine and Mary Lou were pleased. *So am I.*

Kathilu Rader Mote
Christiana Elementary School
Second Grade Teacher

The Precious Gift

I gently unwrapped the tissue of the tiny flat package. The soft, once-white sweater lay lovingly folded in several sheets of tissue. Bunnies played on either side of petite, pearly buttons.

I'm transported back to the first day I ever saw this precious little gift. Grandma Vera had made the sweater when my first child was soon to be born. Boy or girl we did not yet know, and so pink and blue bunnies played on the sweater. When he was born I marveled at this tiny little gift from God. A gift from one mother, unable to keep him, but loving him enough to let someone else become his mother. I lovingly slipped the soft sweater on his tiny arms. Two and a half years later this little sweater would adorn his baby sister.

Now, many years later, they are both grown, his little sister having three children of her own. As each arrived they donned the little bunny sweater. It seemed to me that my son would not have a child of his own to wear Grandma's gift. But God, in His perfect timing, knew the day would come when he would call to say, "Mom, we're having a baby." Now, his child will wear the little bunny sweater. I know as the years pass and all the grandchildren have grown, each will return to retrieve the sweater for their precious gift from God to wear.

Carol Covington
Kittrell Elementary School
Fourth Grade Teacher

Pearls

My father, a career military officer, died just three weeks before Doug and I were married. His absence haunted the occasion and the following memories. He had been a gentle man despite his size and rank, and his many absences from our home had only seemed to intensify his love for his "harem" as he called my mother, my sister and I. Gifts of jewelry from around the world were always presented to my mother on his return, and her jewelry box was full of topaz, amethyst, emeralds, lapis lazuli, and jade. One time, though, he brought a gift for me; it was a string of pearls from Japan. A string of real pearls. My mother had shown me how to gently bite the pearls to test their authenticity, and these did feel gritty. Oh yes, he had brought me real, grown up pearls.

Grief for my father along with the stringed pearls was tucked away for many years. They both traveled safely hidden away as my husband and I were transferred from place to place for the next quarter century. Finally we settled and thrived in a new home, too busy to think with three children, jobs and graduate school until our daughter chose her life's mate and prepared to marry.

The preparations were intense as my beautiful daughter planned the perfect wedding, except for her uncooperative mother who could not find appropriate clothing.

"No Mother, not black."

"No Mother, not white."

"No Mother, not flowered."

"No Mother, not that."

I would bring three or four dresses home from the store and, dissatisfied, carted them all back. I felt ugly in all of them. And then, finally, a simple navy dress was found with an interesting neckline. The sales woman made several suggestions for jewelry and finally stopped, nodded her head and said, "Pearls, yes, you need pearls."

Pearls? I remembered my pearls, and the tight little knot in my heart nudged. I dug the pearls out and tried them on; they were too tight from disuse, like the knot. I sat for a long time and remembered my dad. I could see him—big, strong, tall, gently handing that fragile strand to me, his oldest daughter. I could hear him say "Wear them and be beautiful my daughter."

I had the forty-year-old pearls re-strung and added an enhancer to lengthen them. I felt beautiful. I thought of my dad and how he had loved his girls, his "harem." He had missed my graduation while in Vietnam, died before my wedding, and never met his granddaughter, but my dad would be at my daughter's wedding because I had invited him out of the knot of my heart and back into the family that loved him.

Chris Shafer
LaVergne High School
Ninth Grade English Teacher

Full Circle

While I look at my grandmother's first engagement ring, I am catapulted back to the carefree days of my childhood. The journey carries me to a time in my past when I was known as little "Holly Jo."

As a meddlesome child, I found great pleasure in going to visit my grandmother. An afternoon at Granny's allowed me a freedom that I did not have at home. When I visited my granny, my favorite thing to do was to plunder through her house: closets, cabinets and drawers. I was most in awe of the simple wooden jewelry box that was safely kept on the top of her dresser.

One particular afternoon, Granny must have been napping when I approached the jewelry box, feeling like a pirate who had just discovered a sunken treasure. I warily removed the box from the dresser. It clinked as I lifted it, and it was almost weightless. I opened the box and inspected each and every item carefully. My chubby fingers, with unkempt nails, would become the home for her rings. Her necklaces were an addition to the sweat bead necklaces that I already possessed. I proceeded to the bathroom where I opened the cabinet and located several sample Avon miniature lipsticks, applying a layer of each color. The oversized clip on earrings pinched my ears as I gazed at myself in the mirror, adorned with my Granny's make-up and jewelry.

"Granny, can I have this ring when you die?" I asked in the voice of an innocent, insensitive nine-year-old. I could hear the couch squeak as she arose. Her shoes made a clicking sound on the hardwood floor as she strolled toward the bathroom.

Granny, who was only fifty-nine and in the prime of her life, appeared at the door of the small pastel pink bathroom.

She gazed at the ring on my young hand and with a faraway look in her eyes gave the ever evasive answer, "We'll see."

"Where did you get it?" I inquired further. She peered down at my chubby little hand and saw the ring in question. Her blue eyes twinkled as she stared at the ring. She paused as if she had to think about the answer, but I could tell she was reminiscent of a fond memory that was evoked by the ring. I anxiously awaited her reply.

After what felt like a lifetime, she stated, "Your grandpa gave it to me as my first engagement ring. That was back in 1934." At that moment the ring became more than just a ring to me. It became a symbol of the never-ending love that my grandparents shared.

On November 6, 1976, we received a phone call in the night telling us of my grandfather's untimely death. I was eleven at the time. A few weeks later, while visiting my grandmother, she led me into her room. She gently removed her jewelry box from the dresser. Inside the jewelry box lay the quaint little diamond engagement ring. She looked at me with love in her eyes an said, "Holly Jo, I want you to have this." Granny then placed the ring in my hand. I slowly took the ring and slipped it on my finger. Words would not come. I barely mumbled, "thank you," as my Granny and I hugged.

I am now thirty-five years old and Granny is eighty-four. The ring now rests safely in my wooden jewelry box that is kept on my dresser. It is worn only on special occasions. The Lord has blessed me with meddlesome daughters of my own who love to rummage in closets, cabinets and drawers. Their favorite place to meddle is in my wooden jewelry box.

One morning I entered my bedroom to find my daughters wearing my jewelry to accessorize their outfits. Alicia had on some of my best necklaces and Carley was wearing the ring. Life completed a full circle that day when Carley looked at me and asked, "Momma, where did you get this ring? Can I have it when you die?" I replied, "We'll see."

Holly Smith-Eady
Barfield Elementary School
Fifth Grade Reading and Language Arts Teacher

Memories

Slip one small finger in carefully. Handle the delicate material as if it were a piece of fine china. Do not let the dingy white color, the tattered material, or the missing pearl-shaped button keep you from visualizing the small-framed woman who very proudly slipped one small finger at a time into her soft white gloves as she left for church on Sunday.

Her name was Evelyn Scott, also known as Eve. However, to her grandchildren she was Mammie. This giant of a woman stood less than five feet tall; her frame was frail and crooked. Her hair was as white as snow and her skin slightly wrinkled from age. She had a sweet-sounding voice, and she spoke in almost a whisper. She was a retired cafeteria worker who lived on a large farm in Eagleville, Tennessee.

As a child, I loved to visit her every summer. Helping with daily chores seemed more like a game than work. There was nothing better than running through acre after acre of plush, green farmland, picking bushels of mountain-high beans, or rolling out sticky biscuit dough for supper. Whether we were snapping those beans on a hot summer day in the middle of July on a plantation style porch, making biscuits, or canning the many vegetables we had harvested in a kitchen with ceilings that seemed to reach the sky, we were certainly unaware of the sweat running from our brows or the time ticking away on the clock. Mammie made every chore seem like a Sunday picnic under a big oak tree.

This woman was to me as pure as her gloves were white. I have always treasured the memory of my grandmother. Just as her small fragile hands fit securely into her Sunday gloves, so did her lifestyle fit the era in which she had lived. Mammie was confident with the woman she had become and the things she had accomplished. Raised in a generation of hard workers, discreet, and as much a lady as any "Southern Belle," this small woman carried herself with pride and fit into a society very different from today's.

Her absence from Earth brings a sadness to my heart, but the dingy white gloves remind me of her. I hope I fit into my surroundings as securely as she fit into hers. She is gone but not forgotten. Memories last forever!

Diane Moore
Smyrna Elementary School
Fourth Grade Teacher

My Chantilly

Chantilly. To me it's not a song, a perfume, or even a trendy name for a baby girl, but instead it represents a lifetime of love and family tradition. Momma called me the other day, "It's time; I'm not entertaining as much as I used to, and I know this will cheer you up. Come on over and let's take a look." I had actually dreaded this conversation more than I had realized. I know Mom and Dad are aging, and I'm moving into a new generation, and soon—like it or not. This is all happening too quickly; I'm still young! Surely Mom and Dad aren't in their seventies? Nevertheless, it's true, and here I am driving to collect my inheritance. This must be a dream.

As Mom slowly took out her boxes of silver Chantilly, my heart sank to think back to the days of her sit-down formal dinners in the home where I was raised. Now, as we stood crowded, hovered over the boxes, I knew Mom was right. There would not be as many dinners as there once had been, here in this cramped condominium dining room. As Momma had said more than once, "I still miss my spacious dining room."

I looked at pieces which were held in the hands of my ancestors and used in the "big house" of one of a fading breed of lost family farms—ours, rather my uncle's—with the sale of almost 1,000 acres coming to a close any day. I can just imagine my great-grandmother Pattie as a young bride lovingly having the "R" for Russell engraved on her new silver service. My grandmother, who lived to be 94, would be pleased that her granddaughter, one of five, was carrying the family pattern home—to be used in the modern world where family tradition and morals are still cherished.

Newly wed, I had complained at how sad it was that from all the people invited to share in my nuptials, my husband and I had only received two pieces of Chantilly. Now, over nine years later, it mattered not. I had in my possession silver service which had touched the lips of friends and family close to me as well as many long forgotten or never known.

Mom had said at first, "Choose six of each—the place forks, salad forks, knives; choose a few more of the spoons—I have extras." Before all was said and done, I came home with eight of each, except for ten spoons. She gave me a delicate lemon fork, but she "couldn't let go of the butter knife, sugar shell, or serving spoons just yet". I was grateful for that token—the refusal to let me have all the pieces. It gave me hope that all was not done in her life.

If my great-grandmother Pattie were alive today, would she be proud of my strong sense of doing things "right" in a world of fast food where families hardly ever enjoy a meal together, much less sit a table in the tradition of old? I often wonder and hope that she and my grandmother may watch from Heaven to behold anything that would please their hearts. May I be fortunate enough to stand at the "pearly gates"—Heaven to all the Russells—with my momma and ancestors some day. We could observe with loving affection, watching sweet loved ones carrying on in tradition with our Chantilly—with all its strength, opulence, and simple beauty.

Caroline Coleman Ott
Central Middle School
Eighth Grade Language Arts Teacher

Graham Crackers with Grandy

My grandfather, Captain John Thomas Braswell, has been gone for a long time now. As I touch the smooth leather case of his gentleman's game set, I remember back to what used to be and of times gone by. Times when people sat for hours, happy to be enjoying each other's company and a cool breeze on a sultry summer's day.

Grandy, as I affectionately called him, was an elegant man. He was tall and had beautiful white hair. He loomed way above me, but was so gentle and soft spoken that the distance melted away. Everybody in town respected and admired his intelligence and the graceful man that he was.

I was the apple of my Grandy's eye — his "Katydid". He would always greet me singing K-K-K-Katie, wonderful Katie, and I would run leaping into his arms. I was his favorite — for he knew little girls rather well. My mother was his only child. He loved my brother dearly, but we had a connection. We were two peas in a pod.

My grandfather loved games, especially cards. We played all sorts of games, but would sit for hours playing gin rummy. It was a rare occasion when I was able to conquer the "master." I was being trained by the best, my mother told me.

After our gin rummy sessions, we had a very special ritual. We would fix ourselves an icy glass of milk and grab a box of Keebler's graham crackers. Then we would climb into his old, soft recliner, and snack to our hearts' content. I loved how the graham crackers were so crisp and subtly sweet.

I still love to eat graham crackers and play cards. I cherish the old, now cracked with age, brown leather case that held my Grandy's games. He was given the set while he was in Hawaii during World War II. As I read the gold engraving of his name that appears on the case, I can envision the times he would play the games that the case held. I could see him sitting around the table with the other officers, playing cards and having a cool drink.

I miss him dearly. One day, hopefully, I will have a little child of my own. His name will be John Thomas, and we will play cards and eat graham crackers just like Grandy and I did.

Katherine Wallace
Buchanan Elementary School
Fifth Grade Teacher

The Memory Wreath

Memories are treasures with immeasurable value and they often sustain you and give you a feather-light feeling in your heart when you need it most. My mother told me once that we might never be rich with money, but that we were the richest people on earth because of the experiences we have had and the love we will always remember. Memories have even greater value when you can share them with someone and enjoy the telling of them as you picture in your mind once again that special moment or person. Visual reminders sometimes send me off on a short memory trip and let me feel just for a few minutes the things that have brought me so much joy. My children do not share these memories of my parents and my childhood, so I try to find ways to share little colorful tidbits that will be meaningful to them and also plant images in their minds that they can cherish. This is how the memory wreath came to be at my house.

My children will never know my mother or father, but they love to hear about "the way things were" because it truly was a different time and place. One day it occurred to me to gather some of the little items I have that belonged to Mother and put them together on a wreath that gave or represented a portrait of who she was. It is hanging close to the front door and serves as a stimulus for me to remember experiences and feelings about her and it entices my children to ask about each item. Visitors are also curious about the items I selected and their arrangement on the wreath. Every item there has many stories and I love telling them over and over.

The pale pink gloves remind me of the drawer full of soft, multicolored gloves that I tried on and had tea parties with. Beside the gloves are draped a string of pale artificial pearls and the matching earrings. I can close my eyes even now and see them placed against her favorite lavender dress. She loved to dress up and go to church and other events! The old rusty scissors, thimble and bobbin remind me of the clothes made by loving hands that helped extend the tight budget of a minister's household. The butter knife and teaspoon from her Chantilly silver service that I inherited bring thoughts of all the wonderful meals, family gatherings, and the special guests who continually filled our home. Close to the silver sits a miniature bone china teacup, the last of a beloved collection moved from home to home. This lone survivor tells of the hours spent by a little blond-headed girl who loved tea parties and tiny cups.

The last item is the most special because it is a patch of the quilt from my mother's bed. Mother's twin sister made it of bits and pieces of cloth scraps that might be meaningless to others yet speak volumes to me. The piece of fabric is part of the quilt that covered the bed my mother died in, and I touch this tiny memory each time I pass by and every touch only brings me more happy memories. I hope my children and others continue to ask me about the items since there are so many more stories to tell about the "memory wreath." Maybe one day a "memory wreath" will be created to remember me.

Linda Prichard
Rutherford County
Elementary Instructional Specialist

The Ring

I remember it always sat gracefully on her long, narrow finger (a finger tipped with Chili Pepper red nail polish). It glinted in the light as she worked on fixing her hair or cooking a meal. The rectangular shape and pale, crystal blue color reminded me of looking into a deep pool of water. You could see the history, the story behind it as you looked at it.

My sister and I never tired of hearing the story about it. "Grandma, where did you get that ring?" we'd ask, even though we knew the answer. She'd patiently begin to tell us its story and its future.

"When your father was born the ring was given to me as a gift. Your great, great Aunt Pearl, who never had children, gave it to me. Now it is the beginning of a new family tradition. Your father was my second child, and the ring will be passed to you, his second child, and so on and so forth."

I remember my excitement at being the one blessed to be born second (the only time I viewed that as a blessing). Many years passed, and the ring was always on my grandmother's finger, until last year when she grew weak and ready for a new journey. As God would have it, I learned that I was expecting, after years of infertility. We called my grandmother with the good news. She was so excited, and the nurses said it seemed to improve her spirit. About a month later, she was gone.

The ring now sits on my finger not as gracefully as on hers, but the story is still there to be passed on to future generations.

Carol Tomlinson
Thurman Francis School
Fifth Grade Teacher

Footnote: After receiving the ring we noticed that, turned in the right light, you can see a heart in the middle. My father says that it is my grandmother's heart to carry with me and have forever.

The Precious Pearl Pendant

I can still hear Mom's voice, "You'll have to show me that you can respect things," as she gently placed the small gold ring in my pubescent hand. This was my test. If I could hold onto the ring for an allotted amount of time, then I would be awarded a precious gift on my sixteenth birthday. What Mom failed to realize was how much I would value *any* jewelry!

Being a girly-girl who always looked like a tomboy because of my oh-so trendy Dorothy Hamill haircut and generous stature, I was anxious to possess the things that made Barbie so cool: long hair, high heels, fashionable clothes, and jewelry. I expended lots of energy ensuring that the ring remained on my finger after hand washing or showers. I always double-checked the pool deck or kitchen counter so that I wouldn't inadvertently leave the ring homeless and ruin my chances for the unknown prize.

Of course, in my mind, I had adequately shown ample respect for the ring by the end of the first week. However, weeks turned into months and months into years. My mind became consumed with thoughts of dates, driving, and *boys*. Although I continued to wear the ring every day, I had almost forgotten about the precious gift I had been promised. But as my birthday grew closer, I set my sights on a brilliant blue Honda Prelude. What more precious gift could there be? The day before my birthday, the gleaming Honda disappeared from the lot and I was certain it *was* my precious gift.

I awoke on September nineteenth filled with anticipation as I anxiously awaited the presentation of the precious gift. Mom sashayed into my sanctuary singing "Happy birthday to you, Happy birthday to you," as I sat up in the round king-size bed and leaned against the crushed blue velvet tufted headboard. (What can I say? It was the early eighties!) As Mom gingerly sat on the edge of the bed, she held a small meticulously wrapped box.

Now, you must understand that gift-wrapping is not my mother's strong suit. Often, I received gifts wrapped in grocery bags or the comics from the Sunday newspaper. So, when I saw the glistening gold gift wrap tied with a white fabric ribbon, I immediately became overcome with anticipation of the surprise held in the box. As Mom

66

passed it to me she said, "I know that this will mean as much to you as it does to me. You are such a precious part of my life. I wanted to share this gift with you." Suddenly, my sixteen-year-old brain began to process the words Mom had spoken. In my mind, I heard "I love you, here are the keys to the brilliant blue Honda parked in the..." But then, as if I had been hit in the head with a hammer, the word *share* echoed in my head. As the word bounced around like a five-cent super ball from the bubble gum machine, I tried to justify the reason why Mom would have chosen the word *share*. Maybe it meant that she would enjoy sharing a ride in the brilliant blue Honda. No wait... it had to mean that we would share money to put gas in the brilliant blue Honda. Yes, that must be the reason. Instantly, everything made sense to me, the teenager.

Then Mom placed the beautiful box in my hands. I reverently peeled the sweet golden gift. I gently lifted the shiny white box top. What lay beneath the billowy cotton both astounded and amazed me. However, I cannot remember ever feeling so disappointed. Although the gift was housed in, what I thought, was the perfect car key pouch, it was not a car key at all. Rather, it was a key of different sorts. A key to Mom's long forgotten past. Nestled in the soft, white cotton like a newborn in bunting was a small pearl pendant. "My mother gave this to me when I turned sixteen," Mom whispered, her voice quivering and her eyes filled with tears. Beneath the pendant was a black and white photograph of Mom wearing the pendant and the smile of a younger, happier girl of sixteen. My disappointment quickly evaporated as I cradled the photo in my hands.

I instantly understood the meaning of *precious*. Trust me, it is not a brilliant blue Honda, but rather a precious pearl pendant that coupled two worlds eternally. Even though my heart understood the meaning of *precious*, my brain could only comprehend that I had *not* received the brilliant blue car. I failed to see the pain in Mom's eyes through my self-absorbed fog. It is only now, with a child of my own, that I can clearly see the anguish I caused my mom that day. (I'm certain that it wasn't the only anguish I generated during my turbulent teenage years.)

Though the years continue to expire, I am constantly reminded of the day my relationship with my mom was forever changed. The recollection is unclouded each time I touch the precious pendant that rests gently over my heart.

Sheryl Evans
Rockvale Elementary School
Second Grade Teacher

The Quilts

It wasn't the first or the last. However, it was the first one for me. My grandmother made the quilt just the right size for my bed. On the front, it had the silhouettes of at least twenty little girls with large round bonnets. Each part of each little girl was shaped from a different swatch of fabric. Some swatches were solid, some spotted, and some striped. I chose to use it as the comforter for my bed so it would always be on top and could always be seen. I kept it on my bed for many years until I thought I was too mature for the girlish-looking quilt.

When I went off to college, she made me another quilt just the right size for my dorm room bed. I decorated my entire room around the colors in the quilt. There were pink, green, yellow, and blue pastel pieces.

A few years later, I married. Once again my grandmother made me a quilt; this time just the right size for our bed. My husband often asks me to take the quilt off the bed in the summer. "It's so hot," he says. I'm stubborn about some things. The quilt does not come off. I cherish all the quilts my grandmother has made me. I miss my grandmother.

Lori Thompson
Roy Waldron School
Fourth Grade Teacher

MaWalker's Dishes

Every Christmas Eve before MaWalker died, my father's family gathered to celebrate the holiday together. The table was always set with a white linen tablecloth and my aunt's gleaming silverware and china; surrounding all of this beauty were the myriad of dishes that my aunts and cousins had brought to share with their family. But the most beautiful of all were my grandmother's simple ceramic dishes.

They weren't elegant in the way fine china or crystal or silverware are elegant— they didn't gleam from light refracting through them or from multiple coats of polish. These simple dishes gleamed from my grandmother's pride. I don't know how long she had them, but even as a child, I couldn't miss her connection with them. The children were not allowed to use them because they might easily be broken. I looked but didn't touch; yet still I admired these pale green dishes, the shade of fresh lettuce from a garden in the spring, that brought such a smile to my grandmother's face. Some of the dishes were decorated with translucent ivory cutouts of hearts and flowers; these and a special bowl are the ones I treasured most. They were a part of my grandmother as much as her delectable homemade biscuits and her mouthwatering fried chocolate pies.

The last Christmas Eve before MaWalker died, the biscuits were wrapped in a holiday towel in one of the ceramic serving bowls. I don't think MaWalker made the biscuits that year because she was not in good health, but they were on her table in her dish as part of a family tradition.

MaWalker died when I was only eleven years old. I haven't savored a fried chocolate pie or such a perfect biscuit since — but when I serve a special meal, more often than not, my bread is wrapped in a towel in the green ceramic dish that was my grandmother's.

It's a small tribute to a wonderful lady, but I know in my heart that it is one of the most special ovations that I can give her. Making fried chocolate pies might even be better!

Lois McGonigal
Blackman High School
Ninth Grade English Teacher

Reaching Beyond

Another World

One of my favorite things is relaxing on my back porch on a lazy summer afternoon to read. It might be the newspaper or the latest Oprah book; it doesn't matter. The sun is shining and a soft breeze rustles the thirsty leaves. I extend my legs and prop my feet up. Instantly, I'm whirled into another world. It may be a world that man has already experienced or a world that is yet to be seen. A world where there are no schedules to keep, no suppers to fix, and no sibling arguments that seem to require 911. Gazing outward, billowy clouds and rolling hills surround me. In the distance I see farmers tirelessly tending their fields and smell the exhilarating scent of fresh cut hay. The only sounds I hear are the notes of Tennessee's Mockingbird and the lonely cries of a Rain Dove. Time seems immeasurable, and I become invigorated as I sip on my cool, refreshing lemonade. I feel very light-spirited, almost as if the entire planet has ceased spinning, and I can breathe. Let the world continue with its fast pace. Life doesn't get any better than this. I'm staying here. Then suddenly, without warning, I hear those enduring words, "Mom!" "Mom!" I know instinctively, it's time to leave my serene getaway, and I'm instantly impelled back into the real world.

Mary Beth Walkup
Lascassas Elementary School
Fourth Grade Teacher

I Remember...

I remember hot summers at my grandparent's farm and the absolute pleasure I got gathering the basket of eggs from the chicken house. I can still see the chickens flying around trying to protect their eggs. The air was full of the smell of stale hay.

I remember the devastation I felt in the seventh grade when I was the "only one" not allowed to attend the Michael Jackson concert in Knoxville with my group of friends. My fear of being taunted by my peers was overwhelming.

I remember the summer of 1990 when I met my future husband. We met at Opryland Themepark where we were both ride operators. Our first date followed a long, hot day of working in the busy park. I felt nasty and unattractive, but we immediately fell in love.

I remember my wedding day in 1992 and the feelings that day evoked in me. I see the colors of the green ferns and plants, the white lily flowers, the taste of chocolate cake, and being surrounded by my loving family and friends.

I remember May 13, 1997 and the great joy the birth of my daughter brought to my life. After experiencing fertility problems, my pregnancy and her birth were a blessing. I'll never forget the first moment I held my precious baby girl.

I remember April of 1999 and the deep sadness and empathy I felt after my husband was diagnosed with Type II Diabetes. Dealing with his depression that ensued was a life-altering experience for me.

These memories, or snapshots, of my life evoke many emotions in me. Some bring a smile to my face, and some bring about a chilling, vulnerable feeling in me. I've always wondered why bad things happen to good people, or why some people get all the luck. I may never know, but I am certain that these memories have changed my life and made me a stronger person.

Kim Williams
Rock Springs Elementary School
Third Grade Teacher

The Battle

I remember when I could not lift a heavy twelve-pound bowling ball, much less throw one down a long, narrow alley with ten shiny white pins standing straight and tall as if they were soldiers ready for battle. A battle, that's a good word to describe the game of bowling.

As I enter the smoke filled, brightly lit room, there are children screaming, people talking in voices as loud as thunder, and the intercom cracking as the attendant says, "Would number twenty come to the front desk?"

As I walk slowly toward my lane, I realize the battle is about to begin. I put my dirty white bowling shoes on and carefully lift my dull blue bowling ball from the torn and tattered bag it is kept in. I approach the front line with caution. I prepare for a battle that seems impossible to win. There are voices of encouragement in the background. Lining up my trembling feet on just the right mark is difficult. The mark is a small black dot that becomes a major weapon in my battle against the pins. To aim toward that microscopic arrow approximately fifteen feet away seems to give the pins an advantage, or so it would seem. As I prepare to march into battle, I take a deep breath. I begin to step toward my opponents.

It seems to take an eternity to get to the point of release, also called the foul line. Each step is planned carefully, and I never take my eyes off the arrow. If I miss my mark, the ten pin soldiers will be ahead of me. If I step over the foul line, they will have a definite advantage. They stand at the end of the lane. They are pear-shaped soldiers, and they seem to be saying, "*Come on*, and give it your best shot!" I hear their snarls, their laughter, and they seem to be mocking me. I am determined to win! I have reached that famous point of release. With my arm slowly moving forward and my fingers tightly clutching the bowling ball, I release with a fiery rage.

Pow! I hit the mark! My aim was right on target. The soldiers fell, and I stood in amazement. Each frame required the same approach. With each battle, I felt victorious. The soldiers continued to fall, one by one. With a score of *202, I had won the battle!*

Diane Moore
Smyrna Elementary School
Fourth Grade Teacher

On Writing

You can't make me!
Don't worry I won't try.
It's better to be safe than sorry.

Simply get going, be flexible, and make it fun,
And hear the sound of music in the words.
Keep at it, do something every day.
Don't stop when the rain falls or the snow flies.
Remember I can't make you,
But you can always decide to try!

Carol Tomlinson
Thurman Francis School
Fifth Grade Teacher

A Magical Musician

(words from "Duke Ellington in Person" *American Legacy* Spring 1999
Vol. 5/No. 1)

Abundantly and equally blessed with talent,
Never to have suffered until, perhaps, the very end.
Unfailingly polite and apparently unflappable.
Gliding suavely through a life he called blessed,
Blessing the world with music,
Sounding like nothing before or since…
Duke Ellington, America's greatest musician,
Author of some two thousand compositions from three-minute masterpieces.

Arranged by Renessa Yokley
Riverdale High School
English Teacher, Tenth and Eleventh Grades

Feng Shui

Wind water with cosmic breath
Permeates Earth,
Animates nature's forces,
Combines disparate elements into
One harmonious whole.

Legendary power, fabled energy
Dissolves barriers,
Attracts good fortune,
Provides peace and harmony
To hear the stream with open eyes.

Laurie Jobe Watts
Christiana Elementary School
Fourth Grade Teacher

It's All in the Name

Many attributes useful in teaching
Respectful to all who try
Serious about my profession

Meticulous in all that I do
Organized for sanity
Running an endless race
Goal-oriented and always striving for perfection
Anal about everything
Nourishing to all children

Angi Morgan
McFadden School of Excellence
Fifth Grade Teacher

Wanderlust

Fantasizing about the next trip abroad
Eagerly anticipating the travel section of each Sunday's paper
Recalling the memories of earlier journeys
Never free of the next port of call.

Windjammer Cruises have beckoned for years
Istanbul calls from its minarets and golden domes.
European cities of Florence and Venice tempt with their magnificence
Lorelei sings of Bermuda's beauty
Asia, knowing it has no equal, awaits my return.
New Zealand whispers, reminding that my friend is growing old, and a
Day never passes without this yearning for foreign lands, where I
    relearn that we are one.

Fern Wieland
Rutherford County
K-8 Spectrum Facilitator

Flying Apart

I remember the day I had to leave my future husband for the first time. I met him in college and we dated for almost a year. We had different backgrounds and we came from different states, many miles apart. We knew when summer came we would have to return to our separate homes and our lives would begin to change. With all these changes in store for us, we were unsure of our future together. I still had three years of school while he was graduating and beginning a new life with a new job.

The day inevitably arrived when I had to return home to my family for the summer. We held onto each other all the way to the airport and even to the plane itself. I already had tears in my eyes when the trip began, and I don't think they ever stopped flowing. When we walked to the gate he told the flight attendants I wasn't feeling well and I needed help onto the plane. We were both desperate to hold onto every last second together.

I remember walking toward the plane and feeling the cold, stale, recycled air. It reminded me of an old, stiff piece of cardboard. A distant part of my mind was aware that the smiling faces of the flight attendants slightly changed. Maybe they were remembering a time when they had to separate from someone they loved.

We sat together in the small plane seats and held each other as tightly as we could, until someone came up and said it was time for him to leave. I squeezed him a little tighter, not wanting his warmness to leave, as I cried a little harder. He then gave me one last hug and whispered, in a quiet, shaky voice the words "I love you". He had not spoken these words to me before. I was surprised he said them yet comforted at the same time. He eventually stood up and I noticed he also now had tears in his eyes. At that moment I was overcome with emotion. I had one of those amazing moments; I was happy and sad, but sure of everything at the same time. I knew from that time on, he was going to be the man I would marry.

As the plane left the ground and I was alone, I heard those powerful words repeated in my mind over and over again. I could hear his voice so clearly saying, "I love you, I love you...

For three long years we lived apart. There were many days during those years I thought, "I can't make it any longer." I always remembered this moment and the reasons why we were holding onto each other's hearts. We made it through many hard times and now we are so thankful we are together.

As I look back, even through the sadness, this is one of my favorite memories. I will always hold that day and those special words close to my heart.

Carolee Krajci
Smyrna West School
Kindergarten Teacher

Sally

My grandmother Sally was in her early eighties when she first came to stay. While riding the lawnmower at her house, she fractured her back. This forced her to move into my parents' house. She was only planning to remain until she was able to take care of herself. Little did we know that time would never come.

Once Grandma came to my parents' house, it became quite obvious that something else was happening to her. Forgetful did not even begin to describe her. This was first attributed to all of the medication she was on for pain. After a while, she tried to move back home. It didn't work. Forgetting to take her medicine, forgetting to eat, and lying on the couch forced her to move back in with my parents.

Doctors determined that Grandma was in the beginning stages of Alzheimer's Disease. This was a death sentence for her. My grandfather had passed away more than twenty-five years earlier, and she had become very independent. It was a shock when she could no longer do what she wanted to do, when she wanted to do it.

At first, Grandma was only absent-minded. She would forget to eat, repeat herself, and get confused. The confusion quickly progressed into anger. She did not understand what was happening to her and quickly became the most miserable person I had ever known. If she was at home, she wanted to go out. If she was out, she wanted to be at home. Never content. This was coming from a lady who never complained in front of anyone. It now did not matter who you were; you heard it all. If you would listen, you got an earful.

This time was extremely difficult for my parents. Sally is my dad's mom, and he wanted her to be happy. Whatever he did, it was wrong. She would follow him around the house. "Take me home! Don't you love me? Take me home!" she would viciously attack. As soon as he got home from work, she would start. She knew she wouldn't be able to get to my mom as easily, so she didn't try. This was definitely out of character for her. She had been one of the most loving people anybody could know. She would do anything for anyone before the disease. She had become an evil person. Every once in a while she would realize what she was doing and apologize. She would forget instantly though, and start all over again.

The next stage she went through was self-pity. Who can blame her? Nobody came to visit her, she felt like no one listened to her, and she sometimes realized what was happening to her. She complained all of the time that nobody loved her. Even with my family constantly reinforcing our love, it was never enough for her. Twenty-four hours a day this went on. It was difficult for my dad to watch his vibrant mother deteriorate. She had her moments when she would be completely lucid. This was only a cruel joke to get my dad's hopes up.

Eventually Grandma lost the ability to walk. She became bedbound. This was a constant battle. She could not comprehend that she could not walk, and she constantly tried to struggle out of bed. My parents had a couple of scares when she succeeded. The unhappiness continued. They would get her out of bed and into her wheelchair. As soon as she was settled, she wanted to go to bed. This scenario repeated itself endlessly.

Grandma quickly deteriorated to the point she is at now. She is bed-bound, can't eat solid food, and can't speak. She has started having mini-strokes. She has lost control of her bodily functions and has lost about eighty pounds. She is a living skeleton, resembling a POW from WWII. Whenever I go to visit, I go into her room to see her. I tell her how much I love her and how beautiful she is. She does react to me when I say these things. I think she is trying to answer me, but who knows. To me, she will always be the beautiful person I remember as a child.

Jo Lyn McWhorter
Cedar Grove Elementary School
Sixth Grade Teacher

Shelia

Shelia

Funny, friendly, short, sassy
Who loves reading, movies, cream cheese, and kids
Who hates long checkout lines, thunder storms, diets, and sad endings
Who fears the advancement of time, running out of time, and time outs
Who feels out of sorts when the children change my radio station
Resident of Murfreesboro, Tennessee 37130

Bratton

Shelia Bratton
Rutherford County
Middle Level Coordinator

Regina

Caring, loyal, dependable, persevering
Who loves... God, family, the beach especially at sunrise, watching
young children at play, reading, and chocolate.
Who hates... seeing children being mistreated, witnessing parents *not*
parenting, being late, and snakes.
Who fears... my children being harmed, fire destroying my home,
and growing old alone.
Who feels... joy as I watch my children excel, happiness when
spending time with loved ones, sadness knowing so many elderly
people are alone in this world, and nervous when speaking to
a large group.
Resident of Smyrna, Tennessee

Regina Williamson
Cedar Grove Elementary School
Fourth Grade Teacher

Linda

Linda

Compassionate, Loyal, Funny, Animated

Who loves the countryside and a slow, caring way of life.
Who hates asphalt, concrete, and subdivisions that devour what was
    once a beautiful countryside.
Who fears too many people, industry, and technology.
Who feels very deeply about lov*ed ones.*

Resident of Middle Tennessee, quickly changing from what I first
    loved when I came here.

Postiglione

  Linda Postiglione
  Roy Waldron School
  Third Grade Teacher

Wanda

Walking daily
Always on the go;
Nightly working
Daily planning
Active kindergarten teacher!

  Wanda Jones
  Smyrna West School
  Kindergarten Teacher

Atlas Shrugged: A Character Poem

Driven by a need for justice
Articulate in all situations
Grateful for intellect and diligence
Navigator of a new society
Young in age, but ancient in wisdom and responsibility:

This is the heart of Dagny Taggart.

> Lois McGonigal
> Blackman High School
> Ninth Grade English Teacher

Fahrenheit 451: A Character Poem

Grim builder of blazing infernos
Undermining the world of thought, ideas
Yet driven to stop, to read
Making literature live again.

> Rebecca Robertson
> Blackman High School
> Tenth Grade English Teacher

Shall We Take a Road Trip?

Of the many memories I have from the trip my husband and I took to England last summer, my favorites are from our driving escapades across the English countryside. Everyone knows that driving in Europe is shrouded in the mysteries of steering wheels on the wrong side of the car and cars on the wrong side of the roads. It should be stated that to the Brits and Scots, they *are* driving on the right side of the roads and we Americans drive on the wrong side, but I will leave that debate to another time and place. As seasoned American auto travelers, Ed and I never gave a second thought to any significant obstacle driving in a foreign country could present to us. We never doubted that we had the courage, ability, and wherewithal to overcome any exacerbation as small as driving, conquering the roads of this mere island, and going wherever we wanted. We were armed with AAA maps, Fodor's latest publication on the British Isles, and a plethora of travel and history books. We were prepared for anything.

Ed drove the first day and got lost before we could get out of London. I bit my tongue so as to remain quiet and, on his own, he figured out how to get back to the M (highway), which would take us out of the city. Our initial bravado was a little shaken by this early setback, and we were only slightly intimidated by the idea of driving on the wrong side of the car on the wrong side of the road. As I sat in the front passenger seat, I found myself leaning farther and farther toward the center of the car in the hopes that Ed would drive closer toward the center of the road before the trees on the sides of the road became passengers in the car. Depth perceptions change when riding and driving in swapped seats. In the next few minutes, we were very intimated to the point of paralysis when, unsolicited, the car began to talk to us in a spooky, *2001 Space Odyssey*-ish, computerized voice about traffic delays in and around London and its suburbs. We were initially stunned speechless, then curious, and finally rather indignant, wondering why our American cars didn't talk to us in the States.

Eventually, we settled down and were speeding along as fast as we could go in our little Vauxhall. We weren't sure what the speed limit was because no signs were posted. We only tried to keep up with the rest of the traffic so as to not to get run over, which we realized was a real possibility. Our rental car was a sedan with four doors and a boot, which we asked for so that our luggage wouldn't get "pinched." The rental agency considered the car to be mid-sized with a mid-sized engine; however, Ed and I were sure we had nothing more than two hamsters and a rubber band under the hood. This engine was good because it was fuel-efficient—gasoline cost about $5 a gallon—and bad because it needed extra Flintstones feet to pass another vehicle. I tried not to fall into the tempting yet all-too-comfortable trap of being a harping, side seat driver, but we all know this temptation is great and the flesh is weak. I was sure when it was my turn to drive that I would show my husband and the road who the real driver was. "Oh, what fools these mortals be!" How ironic that we were in Mr. Shakespeare's homeland.

I maneuvered the one-lane roads with no problems. To avoid head-on collisions, I deftly veered to the left into the grass each time I faced an oncoming car avoiding the instinctive American turn to the right. My husband was pleased with my driving on the M because I was maintaining my position with the traffic and staying the course. I parked without hitting anyone or anything. Thank God no parallel parking was required. I stopped jumping out of my skin every time I heard the car intermittently speak that eerie, 1960s voice. I hadn't killed us, any farm animals, farm machinery, pedestrians, taxis, bicyclists, or other cars. I was chugging along like the proverbial engine that could. It seemed as though the Vauxhall and I were invincible. Sadly, my euphoria was rather short-lived. Unfortunately for me, two anomalies of the British highway system existed that absolutely struck fear into my heart after my first encounter with them. They were the roundabout and the dual carriageway.

In America, when two roads intersect, we usually have a two-way stop, a four-way stop, or a traffic light with a variety of square or rectangular highway identification signs from which we may choose to continue our trip. In England, there are any number of roads, which can and do meet at an intersection, which is in the shape of a circle. Accompanying these intersections are signs resembling a giant, mutant octopus with road numbers accompanying their appendages for purposes of identification. These circles or roundabouts are reminiscent of King Arthur's Round Table with his knights in shining armor symbolizing the creatures who must successfully leave the roundabout to travel the wide world righting the injustices against Arthur's loyal subjects. Somehow, though, I don't think the scariest dragon in the entire realm could compare to the terror of maneuvering the labyrinth that is the roundabout.

The roads peel away from the circle like spokes on a bicycle and the cars are flung in the directions of the numerous roads seemingly by centrifugal force. Throwing caution to the wind, leaping into the mass confusion of the orbits of each vehicle and circumnavigating the roundabout without benefit of lane lines is maddening. The random motion of the minute automobiles appears to be utter chaos, and any brave knight venturing into the fray and daring to exit the mass of metal dragons only hopes to leave the maddening circulation at the correct speed, in the correct direction, on the correct exit. For, should there be an errant or imprudent exit, the unlucky knight must re-enter the insane fray again only to repeat the process all over again with the hope of getting it right the second time around—no pun intended. I cannot tell you how many times I had to circumnavigate the same roundabout before I could figure out not only which spoke to exit from, but also how to maneuver the car over to that exit without someone dying. All the while, I was driving around the circle at breakneck speed trying not to hit another car. I wish I had had a video camera on the side of the road to film this vehicular insanity. It would have made a great *Funniest Video*. I knew that if for an instant I looked in the rear view mirror, the Pink Panther would be smiling back at me.

The second anomaly, the dual carriageway, proved to be my undoing as a driver on this little island, for it was this aberration which caused my husband to experience true fear. In the United States, we have yellow lines down the center of a road to indicate a two-lane road. In England, they do not. I assumed that dual meant two lanes and carriageway meant a one way road for there was no yellow line in the middle. Well I was partially correct. It did mean one road with two lanes, but it didn't mean a one way street—it meant a two way street, which just so happened to be a major highway. I thought my poor husband was going to come unglued. He began babbling in some unknown language that I thought he had perhaps learned at the ancient Norman Abbey ruins we had visited the previous afternoon. When he could finally speak a complete English sentence, which I could understand and process, I realized he wanted me to pull over and stop the car. When he was able to breathe normally again, he got out of the car and sat on the side of the road. Ed put his head in his hands and said that he now knew that he had never experienced true terror before, and he never wanted to feel so out of control again. In a surprisingly calm voice, he asked me to give him the car keys. I had to muster all of my strength to not let him see me laugh. He said that he was sorry, but I could not drive any more. It was the funniest thing to see all 6'3" of him so unraveled by all 5'3" of me. He did let me drive again a few days later but only when he slept. I know he didn't see any humor that day, but he does laugh a little about it now. Had he been in my shoes, he would still be making jokes about that day.

We can't wait to go back to England and drive to all the places we didn't get to see the first time. We are even thinking about going to other countries in Europe and renting a car—yes, again. We wonder how we will do in a place where English is not the primary language. What sorts of adventures will we have when we can't read the highway signs? What kind of trouble will we encounter? Knowing the two of us, we should probably save extra money for traffic court!

Barbara K. Wolff
Riverdale High School
Twelfth Grade English Teacher

Virgo

Sexy librarian
Whipping off glasses
Unpinning her bun
Brazenly revealing the Vixen
Virgin, prudish tendencies
Intelligent, Critical, and Hyper-analytical
Sympathetic, Insightful, Humane
They often overlook
Her finer attributes

Sheryl Evans
Rockvale Elementary School
Second Grade Teacher

An Excerpt from "Old Zeb"

"Uncle Walter, this is the most boring summer of my life!"
"Really? Sit down, Lila, and let me tell you a story."

***

It promised to be the most horrible summer of *my* life. My mother had
sent me to my great Aunt Hortensia's; she was a no-nonsense Victorian,
my mother warned.

"Please, Walter," she had pleaded as she boarded me on the train, "try
to rein in that wild imagination of yours."

But she was worse than even *I* could have imagined: Aunt Hortensia
made me eat powdered tea cakes, kiss her friends and wear lilac cologne
in my hair.

I planned my escape every day.

The only good thing about that summer was that Aunt Hortensia lived
in an old brownstone near Boston Harbor. At night I would sit at my
windows at 121 East Longfellow, draw the drapes and watch the big ships
glide in and out of port.

From there, I embarked on the greatest voyage of my life.

It began one night as I spotted a mysterious figure approaching from
the wharf. Old and grizzled, he was bend over like a sack of flour from
the weight of his burden. You see, across his back lay reams of rolled
linen cloth. The cuff of his sleeve flickered as the gold buttons caught the
light from the street lamp. On his head sat the finest cap I had ever seen.
I shivered with excitement. As he slipped his key into the lock of the
house next door, I couldn't believe my luck: my neighbor was probably
a smuggler— better yet, a *pirate*.

Over the following weeks I watched him secretly. All manner of curious
deliveries were made to 122 East Longfellow.

Finally, one morning, I spilled the whole fantastic story to my Aunt
Hortensia as she doused my head with lilac water. Truthfully, I was
hoping it would shock her.

It didn't.

In fact, with one practical lecture she dashed all my great hopes for a summer adventure; not only was he *not* a pirate, she stated sternly, he wasn't even a sailor. Old Zeb, she explained, was a retired merchant who presently made his living making ships in bottles. If he was having deliveries made, she continued, it was certainly none of our business. She ended by saying he was eccentric and was probably *redecorating*.

I can't tell you how disappointed I was; although, frankly, he didn't look like the redecorating type to *me*.

"Well, he may not be a pirate, but whatever he is," I rallied, "I'll bet he doesn't put perfume in his hair!"

"It is not perfume, Walter," she corrected me starchly, "it is *cologne*. Now, not another word. Go out and play."

I was going to tell her that, perfume or cologne, it was still going to get me beat up every ten minutes out on the street, when what should I see but *another* mysterious package being delivered to my neighbor's door.

Reeking, I went outside to play immediately.

No one was around as I strolled toward the parcel. No one saw me peer down at the return address and read the words: BOMBAY, INDIA.

But someone did open the door to Old Zeb's house and I stared straight down at a pair of polished black boots.

"Hello boy, ARE YOU LOST?", a voice thundered...

Carmen Deedy
Children's Author
Workshop Leader

Personal Transformations

I accomplished so much this week. I found that I can teach my peers without feeling intimidated or overwhelmed. Though I have relatively little experience when compared to some of the academy attendees, they took what I had to say as important and relevant. I gained confidence because of that.

I never thought I would gain so much knowledge in one week's time. I learned both personally and professionally ways to make my classroom and students excited about English and writing. There will be at least thirty "new and improved" school days for my students.

I will be going to my classroom next week to make plans for the 2000-2001 school year. (I'm actually excited about spending time in my classroom, and I will be meeting with a co-worker to share my new knowledge!)

WOW! I have learned so much about how my children must feel when asked to generate writing. I will focus on creating quiet, uninterrupted writing time. I will also ensure that the children have ample time to effectively utilize each step of the writing process. It has been wonderful sharing ideas, procedures, and techniques with my professional peers. What an eclectic blend we are, as educators! I will be saddened during the closing remarks when I must say good-bye to the terrific friends I have met during the Writers' Academy.

I would like to thank the academy *for making me a better educator! The Writing Academy was all-around excellent! I have learned more than I ever thought possible. The techniques, tools, ideas, and handouts will all be implemented into my classroom next year and for all the years I may teach language arts and reading.*

This next school year will be my first year to teach Language and Reading. Before this academy I was scared and very intimidated by the new curriculum placement, but now I am excited and prepared to start the year! The presenters were knowledgeable, and the information they taught was great. Not only will I go away with an abundance of strategies, but also with lasting new friendships and fond memories of the experience!

After attending this workshop, I've realized just how very little I know about teaching children to write. I was very impressed with all of the instructors' knowledge and what they did in their classrooms.

It was an inspirational week. I can hardly wait to implement all that I've learned.

I also enjoyed meeting with all of the other teachers and making new friends and helpful contacts.

I've truly enjoyed this week and appreciate all of the hard work that was put into it to make it so wonderful. I've learned many new ways to make the writing process more enjoyable for my students and myself. I've also learned better ways of evaluating their writing, other than the red pen! I also discovered how "difficult" writing can be sometimes and will try to be more understanding with my students! Because of this Writers' Academy, writing will be a pleasurable experience this fall.

I feel that I have come away with a wealth of ideas to use in my classroom. The different strategies for getting students to write were great. The Reporter Story sticks out the most; students get to act like reporters and ask questions about your story.

The materials and books were wonderful. I can't wait to share them with my class.

I found out how to get students excited about writing by getting them to write in a variety of ways. In some ways, they won't even know they're writing! I also learned some excellent ways to have students proofread their papers. I learned how to incorporate and evaluate writing in the classroom. I also learned how to teach and use poetry in the classroom, which I was very excited about.

In Writers' Academy, I gained countless ideas and tools that will be integrated into my classroom. I plan to share some of the knowledge that I gained with my fellow teammates at my school. This will better enable us to incorporate writing across the curriculum.

The materials provided have opened my eyes to new planning and evaluation techniques. I feel more competent in the area *of teaching writing and look forward to having my students writing more in the future.*

I have loved sharing ideas with other teachers. There are so many new ideas and strategies I want to go and try right now.

My thoughts on evaluating students' writing have been transformed this week. One concern I have always had was how to attach a grade to a piece of writing. Students come to me on all different skill levels. My thought was "how do you meet students where they are, move forward with them individually, but still be fair?" That is the fabulous thing about portfolios: students have very tangible evidence of their growth and can be so proud of all they've accomplished.

As I walk back into the classroom this fall I will be carrying a tool bag full of tools to share with my students to help them become budding writers. At the same time, their uniqueness and simplicity of ideas will help me to become a better writer.

Before this academy, I was the teacher who knew writing had to be taught but took no joys in it. Frankly, I dreaded it like a plague. I had never had good experiences with writing and was extremely insecure about my own writing.

Now, because of such a wonderful experience in this academy, I have the information and the steps necessary to improve my own abilities and to teach these skills in a creative and positive manner. I can identify with frustrated students and hope to start the same fire in them that has been lit in me this week. I look forward to using many of these ideas in my classroom.

I really believe that I have been transformed as not only a writer but also a teacher of writers.

I learned the skills and techniques to teach writing workshops in college; however, many uncertainties lingered. This week, I believe I gained the confidence that I had lacked before. I gained my confidence in seeing real lessons and ideas but most of all by seeing my concerns and fears being shared with my colleagues and talking through them together. This made a difference.

When I began this academy I didn't know what to expect. I teach kindergarten, so I have the children at the beginning of the writing process. I feel I have gained ideas to assist my students in becoming creative, which will help them when they begin writing.

I also feel the academy helped me personally. I have become more comfortable with my writing and the process. I also have begun a "grateful journal," and I am very excited about it! Thank you for all the knowledge you all shared.

Writing is a process; we only have to look at a 'grammar book' these days to know that. But what I have seen this week is that teaching writing *is also a process full of exciting, fun ideas that should produce much better results than I have gotten so far. I know I can trust teachers of the younger students to prepare the students for high school. I look forward to collaborating with those teachers so that I might be a better teacher.*

I certainly gained new ideas from the Writers' Academy. I was afraid, since I've been using a writing workshop for years, I wouldn't hear anything new. I was wrong. I learned new ways to work with students to develop their own ideas. Working in a group certainly helped me develop my own ideas. Learning to revise my own writing will improve my students' revising skills. I always try to write when my students write, although I'm rarely successful. I will now find my own time to write.

The Writers' Academy has certainly fulfilled my expectations. I love to write, and after a week at this wonderful academy, I am more motivated than ever! I believe writing is crucial. All children have the ability to express themselves in one form or another. As educators, our challenge is finding and enhancing that special writing ability in each child. Thank you for the marvelous ideas.

I have decided to finish all of the pieces of writing I've started during the Writers' Academy and make an example book for my students to use. I feel that transformation has taken place because I am more motivated to write, and anyone can write, right? All you need is a place, paper, pencil, and, most importantly, your thoughts and memories. Thanks for a great week.

As a result of this week, I have become much more sure of my abilities and have gained a wealth of information to take back to my school. My students will be writers, because, even at second grade level, they will be able to feel successful as I use the materials and lessons I bring to them.

A big thanks to those responsible for initiating and putting together a wonderful experience for teachers.

I learned many techniques and methods I will be using with my early writers. Two techniques/ideas I have gained from the workshop which stand out are the use of writing rubrics to evaluate students' work and the many easy formulas for writing poetry. I was very inspired when learning about the ways to get students reading and writing their own poetry. I will definitely be taking these ideas back to my classroom.

I was very apprehensive about teaching writing in my classroom. I didn't do a good job writing, so how could I teach them to write? For this reason I was also nervous about this workshop. I didn't enjoy writing. My whole attitude toward writing has changed. I now enjoy it and can hardly wait to start poetry with my students. I'll incorporate a writers' workshop in my class and each child will keep a journal. Thank you for a tremendous week.

I feel better about approaching creative writing, especially in poetry. All of the sessions encouraged me to think of different, unique ways to inspire students to write on!

This was the best workshop I have ever attended in many ways. The speakers were knowledgeable and interesting. The ideas that they presented were real. That is, they were practical for me as well as for my students. The materials that we received were an unexpected delight. Something new and useful was added each day to a considerable supply given on the first day. Possibly most personally rewarding, was the interaction with fellow teachers. I believe that this was the greatest group of teachers that I have ever had the opportunity to join. They were open, friendly, helpful, and enthusiastic.

I realize that I am going to have to write myself to be able to help my students. The problems I have had this week are the same kinds of problems they have in my class. I have learned new techniques and ideas from the other teachers here. I have so many things I want to change for next year. I can't wait. It has been a wonderful week! Thank you!

I have learned so much this week! Teachers who have tried different strategies and found what works (or what doesn't work) are so helpful to us. I enjoyed the hands-on book-making ideas. This entire workshop has made me really think and believe, we all really do *have a book inside us — it's just knowing how to delve into ourselves to find it."*

Coming to this week-long workshop gave me inspiration not only to teach my students better writing skills, but for me personally to write more. I have ideas on how to make writing more interesting which, in turn, will motivate my students. I have also learned numerous strategies and techniques I know will help me prepare my students for the fourth grade writing test. I didn't know I would leave this workshop with the new-found feelings I have for poetry. I cannot wait to incorporate the projects and activities into my curriculum next year. Writing will be so much more exciting for my fourth graders next year. Thanks!

"Transformations..." as I sit thinking back over the week I think that one word says it all. Writing transforms us physically, mentally, and spiritually.

I think this week has transformed me from a timid, under-confident writer to a confident, eager writer. I have been transformed from a writer of short poems (my comfort zone) to a writer of short stories! I feel blessed that we as people have been given the gift of writing to express ourselves.

I hope to bring out a transformation in my students next year. I hope my enthusiasm will bring out the 'I can' in them.

This has been a wonderful week. I have been inundated with specific ideas that I can take and use in my classroom immediately. I have also been able to experience the anguish of getting that perfect word or phrase down on paper in order to get my message across; this is my shared experience with my students. I love to write— I have always loved to write. This week has rekindled my desire to give purpose and audience to my writing. Thanks so much for this opportunity.

I have gained confidence in my ability to teach writing by attending the Writers' Academy. I have always been hesitant to show my students an end product (they like to select the same topic I share!). By using more of my own writing products in the classroom, I hope to help students feel more confident in their own abilities.

I feel so 'pumped' that I wish school was starting tomorrow. Thanks for the motivation to be a writer and encourage others to do likewise.

I came to the 'first-ever' Rutherford County Writers' Academy with the expectation that I would learn better strategies that would enable me to become a stronger teacher *of writing, certainly* not *to write* myself! *To my surprise and delight, I was* transformed *from a reluctant, insecure writer into not only a more confident teacher of writing, but also a writer myself. Thank you!*

I reached all of my goals this week. I was given so many ideas and techniques that I will have a very hard time deciding what to work on first! I met my goal to become a better writer myself, by reflecting, peer tutoring, and practice, practice, practice! I thoroughly enjoyed every day of the academy and will recommend it to all of my colleagues. I can't wait to be able to implement everything I have learned this week.

I've learned many valuable and practical ways to inspire students to write and to improve their skills. The magic of writing is powerful in our lives!

I'm glad I chose to attend the Writers' Academy. I have taken away from it a renewed spirit and love for writing that sometimes gets lost in the "daily grind." I intend to explore *my own ideas in writing more. The more I write, the more comfortable I become in teaching writing.*

I knew it before, but somehow I had managed to fool myself. Writing is difficult. I have come to appreciate the struggles that all writers face. I came to the academy to become a better writing teacher, but I'm leaving as a better writer.

Poetry, prose and even structural lessons on grammar have opened avenues of teaching and learning strategies for me and my students.

Thanks, academy staff, for the "write" stuff!

The strategies presented were excellent! Some were fresh and different, some were new twists on old strategies. I plan to use many of the ideas in my classroom this year.

I was thrilled to get to know new friends. Perhaps, in a contradictory way, their talents have created a bit of comfort with a sprinkling of discomfort. Can I be as motivating as they?

This Academy was the medication I needed to challenge me to cure the ills of despondency, desperation, and deterioration caused by "The Write Stuff" not happening.

Absolutely fabulous! This has given me the confidence to actually teach writing. Thanks for the wonderful, creative ideas that were modeled.

Thank you, thank you! The core teachers were outstanding. My goals were to find information that I could use in my classroom this year. I did!

I learned how hard it is to write with a time limit. I have never given one in my classroom (with exception—research) and it made me glad that I didn't do that. I really appreciate the "monitor and adjusting" you did to let us get finished.

I wish that more teachers could be here and experience the Writers' Academy.

The Rutherford County Writers' Academy was a wonderful experience for me. Everything I had hoped to learn, I did. I learned inventive, creative ways to teach writing. I also enjoyed the interaction and ideas from other teachers. What a great week!

I have successfully achieved all of my goals and much, much more. I have gotten endless ideas to take back to the classroom. I cannot wait to implement everything I've learned from this academy. This has added to my already enthusiastic attitude toward next year."

What I gained:
Wonderful ideas from so many terrific teachers.
The chance to have a community of writers working
together.
I was able to write poetry and you let me sing!
I had another wonderful learning experience—
Thanks for all you do for our professional development.
Knowing we have such support keeps me energized
and excited about teaching and learning.

I feel I have gained a better sense of direction in teaching poetry and assessing students' written work. I believe this coming year will be an exciting writing experience for me and my students because of what I've learned from the academy.

This week has exceeded my expectations for the Writers' Academy. All the materials, books, breakout sessions, handouts, etc., were great! Hopefully, Rutherford County will be able to have this every year. Word of mouth should travel fast.

To publish a book for your school or not-for-profit organization that complements your academic and financial goals, please contact

WRITE TOGETHER™ PUBLISHING

4064 Nolensville Road
Private Mailbox #342
Nashville, TN 37211

Phone: 615-781-1518
Fax: 520-223-4850

www.writetogether.com
fundraising@writetogether.com